FIRED UP IN FIRECREEK

JUN - 2 2000

FIC
ROBER
PB

Roberts, J. R.
End of the trail.

discard

DON'T MISS THESE
ALL-ACTION WESTERN SERIES
FROM THE BERKLEY PUBLISHING GROUP

THE GUNSMITH by J. R. Roberts
Clint Adams was a legend among lawmen, outlaws, and ladies. They called him . . . the Gunsmith.

LONGARM by Tabor Evans
The popular long-running series about U.S. Deputy Marshal Long—his life, his loves, his fight for justice.

SLOCUM by Jake Logan
Today's longest-running action Western. John Slocum rides a deadly trail of hot blood and cold steel.

BUSHWHACKERS by B. J. Lanagan
An action-packed series by the creators of Longarm! The rousing adventures of the most brutal gang of cutthroats ever assembled—Quantrill's Raiders.

DIAMONDBACK by Guy Brewer
Dex Yancey is Diamondback, a southern gentleman turned con man when his brother cheats him out of the family fortune. Ladies love him. Gamblers hate him. But nobody pulls one over on Dex . . .

WILDGUN by Jack Hanson
Will Barlow's continuing search for his daughter, kidnapped by the Blackfeet Indians who slaughtered the rest of his family.

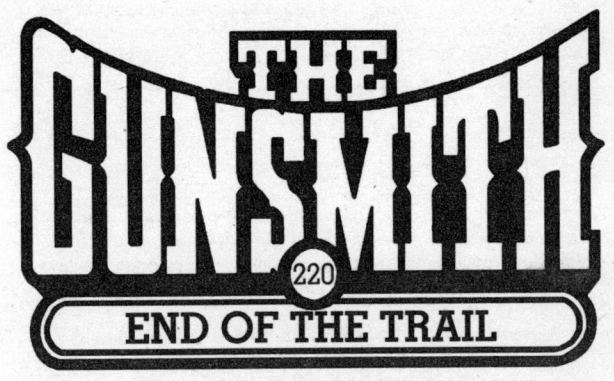

END OF THE TRAIL

J. R. ROBERTS

JOVE BOOKS, NEW YORK

If you purchased this book without a cover, you should be aware that this book is stolen property. It was reported as "unsold and destroyed" to the publisher and neither the author nor the publisher has received any payment for this "stripped book."

This is a work of fiction. Names, characters, places, and incidents are either the product of the author's imagination or are used fictitiously, and any resemblance to actual persons, living or dead, business establishments, events, or locales is entirely coincidental.

END OF THE TRAIL

A Jove Book / published by arrangement with
the author

PRINTING HISTORY
Jove edition / April 2000

All rights reserved.
Copyright © 2000 by Robert J. Randisi.
This book may not be reproduced in whole or in part,
by mimeograph or any other means, without permission.
For information address: The Berkley Publishing Group,
a division of Penguin Putnam Inc.,
375 Hudson Street, New York, New York 10014.

The Penguin Putnam Inc. World Wide Web site address is
http://www.penguinputnam.com

ISBN: 0-515-12791-4

A JOVE BOOK®
Jove Books are published by The Berkley Publishing Group,
a division of Penguin Putnam Inc.,
375 Hudson Street, New York, New York 10014.
JOVE and the "J" design
are trademarks belonging to Penguin Putnam Inc.

PRINTED IN THE UNITED STATES OF AMERICA

10 9 8 7 6 5 4 3 2 1

ONE

Clint Adams was concerned. There was apparently a problem with Duke, his big black gelding. They'd had to stop several times during the week for Duke to rest, something that was totally out of the ordinary. Usually, the gelding had the stamina of a steam engine.

Camped on this night Clint did as thorough an examination of the horse as he could, but could not find anything physically wrong with him.

"What's the problem, big boy?" he asked, rubbing Duke's massive neck. "I sure wish you could talk and tell me. You feeling poorly? Is that it?"

Clint decided that they would stop in the next town and see if there was a vet available. That would be a place called Star Forks, Nevada. He'd never been there, but all indications over the past few days were that it was a fair-sized town, one that should have a vet.

Clint turned in for the night, determined to rise early the next morning, skip breakfast, and get Duke to Star Forks.

In the morning the gelding didn't seem much better. The night's rest had not done him any good. Clint became concerned about riding him and decided to walk him to town. Star Forks, however, was a fair walk from where they were. He hoped that somewhere along the way they'd find a small town where they could stop and maybe use a telegraph to send for a vet.

After several hours of walking, Duke's breathing seemed labored. His big sides were heaving as he tried to catch his breath. Clint was starting to fear that there was something seriously wrong with his big partner, and that he might not make it to the next town. That was when he saw it. It wasn't much of a town, just a few buildings and what looked like one street. There was a large structure at the end of the street, though, that looked like a livery.

"Come on, big fella," Clint said, rubbing Duke's nose, "just a little farther. You can do it."

He did . . . but just barely.

The town was called Firecreek. It was even smaller than he thought, but there *was* a large livery stable at the end of its one street. By the time they reached it Duke's head was hanging down and his breathing was coming raggedly. Clint was afraid that if there was no vet in town the gelding would die.

"Hello the livery!" he shouted. "I've got an emergency here!"

He waited several moments and then a boy of about seventeen appeared, wiping his hands on the back of his britches.

"Can I help ya?"

"My horse is sick," Clint said. "Can you look at him?"

"Oh, I ain't—I don't know nothin' about that," the boy said, and Clint suddenly had the impression that he was not right in the head. Not addled, exactly, but not all there. "We do have a really good vet in town, though. Doc Fuller."

"Will you run and get him quick, then?" Clint asked. "I'll get him unsaddled."

"Doc Fuller ain't exactly—"

"I'll pay him whatever he wants," Clint said. "Just get him over here fast!"

The boy eyed Duke and said, "Sure is a mighty fine lookin' animal," and then took off running before Clint could bark at him again.

Clint had Duke unsaddled and was trying to soothe him when the boy reappeared with a woman in tow. She was a handsome blonde, maybe forty, well built, with her hair pinned behind her head.

"I thought you were getting the vet," Clint said.

"I-I did," the boy said. "I was tryin' ta tell you Doc Fuller wasn't no man. She's a she."

"I can see that," Clint said. "Forgive me, doctor."

"Don't mention it," she said, in a deep, well modulated voice. "I can see you're worried, and from the looks of your animal, probably with good reason. Now get out."

"W-what?" Clint asked.

"Out."

Clint stared at her.

"I want to examine my patient without you looking over my shoulder. I don't work well while being watched."

"Doc—"

"Out, or your horse may be the one who pays the price."

"All right," Clint said. "All right, just . . . take care of him."

"I'll do my best."

The doctor was rolling up her sleeves as Clint and the livery boy went out the door.

Outside the boy said, "Don't worry. Doc Fuller's the best damn vet in the county."

"Is that right?"

"It don't matter none that she's a woman," the boy said. "She's real good with animals."

"What's your name?"

"Petey."

"Well, Petey," Clint said, "I hope you're right."

TWO

Clint waited outside the livery while Doc Fuller examined Duke, and Petey waited with him. After a few attempts at conversation, though, the chatty young man decided to keep quiet. Maybe he wasn't quite as dumb as he had seemed at first.

At one point Doc Fuller came out, wiping her hands on a cloth.

"How is he?" Clint asked.

"You might want to go and get something to eat," she said. "This could take a while."

"Why? What's wrong?"

"He's having trouble breathing."

"I knew that much," Clint said. "What is it you're not telling me?"

"Let me ask you something first?"

"Okay."

"Is this just a horse to you? I mean, is he just transportation, or something more?"

"Something more," Clint said, "much, much more, doctor. He's my friend, my partner, he's saved my life—"

"I had that impression," she said. "I just wanted to make sure."

"What gave you that impression?" he asked.

"Well, for one thing, the way you always refer to the horse as 'him,' and not as 'it.' Most men don't do that."

"Well, Duke is a 'him'," Clint said. "I've spent more time in his company over the years than with any human."

"We haven't really been introduced," she said. "I'm Abigail Fuller—or Abby."

"I'm Clint Adams."

She stopped wiping her hands for a moment, then continued.

"I see," she said. "I think I understand now."

"Understand what?"

"I know your reputation, Mr. Adams," she said, "and I've heard stories about your horse. I should have guessed when you called him Duke."

"So what does that mean, now?"

"It means I truly understand how you feel about your horse," she said. "I have to be honest with you."

"I was hoping you would be."

"There's a chance he might die," she said. "There's a blockage in his esophagus—his breathing passage—"

"I know what an esophagus is, Doctor," he said. "Can't you clear it out?"

"I could if it was a thing," she said, "but it's not something I can pry out . . . it's a growth."

"How does that happen?"

"A few different ways," she said, "but I don't want to take the time to explain it now. I have to get back in there."

"Can you . . . shrink the growth? Is that what it would take?"

"That's what it would take," she said, nodding. "If I can do it, I can save him, but if I can't . . ."

"I understand."

"This is not something that is beyond my capabilities, Mr. Adams," she hastened to add. "I've done it before, but

END OF THE TRAIL

there were other times when I was unable to. I can't make an guarantees."

"The only guarantee I expect, Doctor, is that you'll do your best."

"Abby," she said, "and I will."

"All right, Abby," he said. "I'm Clint, and I'll take you at your word."

"You're going to be here for some time," she said. "You'd better get yourself settled in the hotel."

"There's a hotel?"

"Not much of one," she admitted, "but Petey will show you where it is."

"All right."

"Get yourself something to eat, too."

"Can I bring back something for you?"

"That's kind of you," she said, "but after Petey shows you to the hotel I'll have him run and get me something."

"All right."

"There's one other thing."

"What's that?"

"He's not a young horse."

"I know that."

"If I can pull him through this," she said, "I don't know that you'll be able to ride him. He might have to be put out to pasture."

"I don't care," Clint said. "Pull him through and I'll find the best home for him I can."

"All right," she said. "I'd better get back. He was resting comfortably, but he can go into convulsions at any time."

"Can I come in and get my saddlebags, and see him?"

"Just for a minute."

She opened the door and stepped into the livery, and Clint followed. He was surprised to find the big gelding down on the ground, off his feet. He hadn't seen Duke like that since the time he'd been shot. It had taken a good vet to pull him through that time, too.

Clint knelt down by Duke and touched his neck. The big gelding's eye rolled to look at him, but he didn't move.

"You take it easy, big fella," Clint said. "You do everything the doc tells you."

Duke's eye closed. He was breathing shallowly.

"You better go," she said.

He picked up his saddlebags and rifle and took one more look at Duke, hoping that it would not be the last time he would see his big pard alive.

THREE

Abby Fuller was right about the hotel. It wasn't much, but it did have a room for Clint. In fact, it had four rooms, all of them empty.

The clerk behind the desk was in his fifties, and grinned from ear to ear while pushing the register in front of Clint.

"You can have your pick," the clerk said, happy to have a guest.

"Doesn't seem to be many people around," Clint said, as he signed the register.

"Well," the clerk said, "there's me, and Petey, and Doc Fuller. There's Ben Pepper and his family."

"Who's Ben Pepper?"

"He owns the general store," the clerk said, "and he's our part-time sheriff. He's got a wife and two kids—a son and a daughter."

"Nobody else?"

"Oh, we got a few others," the man said. "Some merchants, the preacher, and then there's the folks who live on ranches in the area. They come to town from time to time to go to church, and shop at the general store."

"Nice, quiet place, then," Clint said.

"Real quiet." He handed Clint his key. "My name's Randolph, but most folks just call me Randy."

Randy and Petey, Clint thought. *Real cute.*

"If there's anything I can do, just give me a holler."

"Is there a place where I can get something to eat?" Clint asked. The man hadn't mentioned a café.

"Last building south of town," Randy said. "It's a rooming house, and Mrs. Bradford prepares meals."

"Even if I'm not staying there?"

"Nobody ever stays there," the clerk said, "but she'll cook whatever you want."

"Fine," Clint said, realizing he was hungry. "I could use a steak."

"Tell her I sent you over."

"I'll do that."

All four of the hotel rooms were on the ground floor. Clint walked through a curtained doorway and found his, room four. It was little more than a bed and a flimsy chest of drawers. He tossed his saddlebags and rifle on the bed and then left to go and find that steak.

When he reached the rooming house the clerk had told him about Petey was just leaving, carrying a tray.

"Food for the doc," he said.

"I see."

"Don't worry," the boy said. "She'll pull your horse through for ya."

"I hope so," Clint said. "Thanks."

"Gotta bring 'er her food," Petey said, and hurried away.

Clint walked to the door and knocked. A woman in her late thirties answered the door, wiping her hands on her apron. She reminded him of Doc Fuller, attractive and competent looking.

"Help ya?"

"I was told over at the hotel that you would prepare a meal for me?"

"You the fella with the sick horse?"

"That's right."

"Come on in," she said. "I'll fix you anything you're willin' to pay for."

"That's fine," he said. "Would a steak be too much trouble?"

"No trouble," she answered. "Like I said, whatever you're willin' to pay for. Come into the kitchen."

He followed her through a sparsely furnished living room into the kitchen, which smelled of coffee and frying meat.

"Just fixed the doc something to keep her goin'," the woman said. "How about some coffee?"

"That sounds great. Uh, you are Mrs. Bradford, aren't you?"

"That's who I am," Mrs. Bradford said. "Have a seat and I'll pour you some coffee."

She gave him his coffee and then dropped a hunk of meat into a frying pan.

"What's wrong with your horse?" she asked, over her shoulder.

"He's having trouble breathing."

"Well," she said, "if he can be fixed Abby's the one to do it. Best damn vet I ever saw."

"That's good to hear."

"Onions?"

"Please."

"And some potatoes?"

"Sounds good."

Delicious smells soon filled the room and then she placed a steaming plate in front of him.

"I appreciate this."

"Be a dollar," she said.

He went for his pocket, but she stopped him.

"After you finish is time enough," she said. "I got some other chores to do. I'll be back to give you some more coffee."

"Thank you, Mrs. Bradford."

She went to the door, then turned and said, "Don't worry about your horse. Abby'll bring him around," before she left.

"I hope so," he said, to nobody.

FOUR

Cord Hardin and his gang looked down at Firecreek. During their last job Hardin had been thrown from his horse. He'd landed hard, but had been able to get up, mount up and escape. That had been two days ago. Now every step his horse took felt like a knife in his side.

"That's a town?" Johnny Tolan asked.

Hardin answered without looking at Tolan.

"It suits our needs."

"What needs?"

"We need a place to heal."

Tolan snorted, but then he was uninjured. Ben Packer had taken a bullet through his arm, and Will Taylor still had a bullet in his thigh. They'd managed to stop Packer's bleeding, but they had to get that slug out of Taylor's leg before the wound became infected.

"They got a doctor?" Taylor asked, doubtfully.

"Not a doctor," Hardin said, "but a damned good vet."

"I ain't lettin' no horse doctor cut me," Taylor complained.

"Fine," Hardin said, "then you'll just lose the leg."

Taylor just scowled.

The other two men—Quinn Butler and Ed Powell—were also uninjured, but were willing to go along with whatever Hardin wanted to do. Johnny Tolan was the only one who didn't want to stop.

"How do you know so much about this little town and their vet, anyway?" he asked.

This time Hardin looked at him with cold, flat eyes.

"The vet and me are old friends."

Clint thanked Mrs. Bradford for the meal and the coffee, both of which were excellent.

"You get tired of sleeping on one of those pallets they call beds over at the hotel you come and stay here," she said. "I got real mattresses."

"I'll remember that," he said, and left.

He walked back over to the livery, found Petey sitting outside. When the boy saw him he stood up, quickly.

"You supposed to warn her when I show up?" he asked.

"Uh..."

"She doesn't want me walking in there, does she?"

"Uh..." Petey looked confused.

"Okay," Clint said, before the look could turn to one of panic, "why don't you go in and tell her I'm here?"

"Uh... okay."

Clint waited and moments later Doc Fuller came out.

"I've got nothing to tell you right now, Mr. Adams."

"Clint."

"Clint," she said. "I'm still working with him. In fact, I think I'll be here all night."

"Will he last that long?"

"I think if I can get him through the night," she said, "he should make it."

"Are you having trouble keeping him calm?" he asked. "He doesn't take to a lot of people, and I thought maybe I could—"

"Duke and I are getting along fine, Clint," she said, patiently. "Why don't you just go and get some rest? You look exhausted."

"I am," he confessed. "I had to walk a long way to get him here."

"Walking him here instead of trying to ride him probably saved his life," she said.

"Well, at least I did something right."

She crossed her arms and looked at him.

"What's that mean? You think you did something wrong that caused this?" she asked.

"What did I do right?"

"You got him here to me," she said. "I don't know of any other vet who could have kept him alive this long, let alone get him through the night."

"So it wasn't something I did?" he asked. "Pushing him too hard, riding too long without rest—"

"This would have happened no matter what, Clint," Abby said. "Stop being so hard on yourself."

"I just thought—"

"Get some rest and stop thinking," she said. "That's what I prescribe for you. Now let me get back to my patient."

"You're going to stay here all night with him?"

"Right by his side, every second."

"I appreciate that, Abby."

"Wait until you get my bill."

She turned and went back inside. She seemed pretty optimistic about pulling Duke through the night, so for the first time Clint started thinking about what he was going to do after Duke was healed. Where should he take him? And what was he going to do for a horse after good ol' Duke was put out to pasture?

It was funny. He knew that the big gelding couldn't go on forever, but he had simply never really thought about what he would do when it happened. After riding Duke for so long what would it feel like to be without him? To be riding another horse? Or was this a sign that maybe his days of riding the trail should come to an end? Should he be put out to pasture at the same time, and in the same place?

He decided to sleep on these decisions and see what came to mind in the morning.

FIVE

The Hardin gang rode into Firecreek, largely unnoticed. That suited Cord and the rest, except for Johnny Tolan, who liked being noticed.

"Where the hell are the people?" he groused. "Shit, what kinda town is this, with no people?"

"Give your mouth a rest, Johnny," Hardin said.

"He's just pissed that a town this size ain't gonna have a cathouse, boss," Butler said, and Powell laughed.

"Shut up!" Tolan growled.

"I'm scared, Johnny," Butler said.

"You should be."

"That's enough," Hardin said. "All of you just shut up. Where's the damn hotel in this town?"

At this point one person appeared, a young boy who was crossing the street. They couldn't tell where he came from or where he was going because none of the buildings were marked.

"Hey, boy!" Tolan shouted.

The boy stopped short, right in the middle of the street, and waited while the six men rode up to him. He looked up at them with wide, totally innocent eyes that reminded

Hardin of the eyes of a dog just before it gets kicked.

"Where is everybody, boy?" Hardin asked.

"Ain't that many people livin' here."

"Well, is there a hotel?"

"Sure is," the boy said. "Got four rooms—well, three now 'cause one of them's taken."

"Four rooms, huh?" Tolan asked. "Whoo, that's a lot of rooms."

"Anyplace else to stay?" Hardin asked.

"Mrs. Bradford's rooming house at the south end of town."

"And someplace to eat?"

"Mrs. Bradford's."

"Where's the livery?" Tolan asked.

"Right at the end of this street. Just keep goin', ya can't miss it."

"All right," Hardin said. "Much obliged, boy. You can keep doin' what you were doin' now."

Without a word the boy continued his run across the street.

"What a half wit," Johnny Tolan said.

"You boys can split up the three rooms at the hotel," Hardin said. "I'm going to the rooming house."

"Hey," Tolan said. "The rooming house is bound to have better beds and food."

"That's why I'm going there."

"Why can't we all go there?" Tolan asked.

"I don't want you all there," Hardin said. "I want to get some rest, so you boys will go to the hotel, like I said. Butler, come with me to the rooming house. I want you to take my horse to the livery."

"Sure, Cord."

"Butler will meet the rest of you at the hotel and then you can get the horses taken care of."

As Hardin and Butler separated from the others he was

aware that Tolan was still griping, but he ignored it. Sooner or later, he thought, he was going to have to get rid of Tolan. He just didn't fit in with the rest of the gang.

When they reached the rooming house Hardin painfully dismounted and handed the reins to Butler.

"Want me to stay while you get settled?" Butler asked.

Hardin removed his saddlebags from his horse and said, "No, that's okay. I can get myself settled."

"Okay, boss. Then I'll see you later."

"Quinn, let me know what Johnny's sayin' when I'm not around, okay?" Hardin said.

"Sure, boss, I'll let you know. You know you can count on me."

"Thanks."

"What should we do about Ben's leg?"

"Just get him settled in a room and I'll have the vet come over and take a look."

"Any chance she won't want to do it?"

"Oh," Hardin said, "I know she ain't gonna want to do it—but she will."

Butler rode off while Hardin walked up to the front door of the house and knocked. The woman who answered was handsome and, while not overly friendly, was pleasant enough.

"Help ya?" she asked.

"I understand you have rooms?"

"I do," she said. "Just for you?"

"Just me."

"I thought I heard two voices . . ."

Hardin smiled and said, "It's just me."

"Well, come in then and I'll show you the rooms. You can have your choice, since no one else—"

"That's all right, Ma'am," Hardin said, "you pick it. I just need to get off my feet."

As he entered she frowned and asked, "Are you hurt?"

"I was thrown by my horse a couple of days ago," he said. "Might have a cracked rib or two."

"I'm sorry," she said. "I wish we had a doctor in town."

"It's okay, Ma'am—"

"Bradford, is my name," she said. "Mrs. Bradford."

"If you would just show me to a room, Mrs. Bradford," he said, "I'll get off my feet for a while. That will do wonders for me."

"Very well, Mr. . . . ."

"Hardin."

"Mr. Hardin," she said. "Just come this way."

SIX

Clint frowned when there was a knock on the door of his hotel room. He wondered if it was the vet, Abby Fuller, with bad news about Duke. When he opened it, however, it was Petey, standing there fidgeting from one foot to the other. Would she send him with bad news? He didn't think so.

"I thought you should know," Petey said, immediately, "that six men just rode into town."

"Why should I know that, Petey?" he asked. "Don't you have a part-time sheriff in town?"

"Sure we do, but I ain't so stupid I don't know who you are, Mr. Adams," the boy said.

"Oh?"

"I knew you were the Gunsmith soon as I heard your name," he said. "These look like bad men, so I wanted to let you know."

"What makes you think they're bad men?"

"Some of them is shot up," the boy said, "and the leader, he's holdin' his side. Couldn't see how hurt he was, but one had a bandaged arm and another one a bandaged leg."

"They're going to be looking for a doctor," Clint said.

"We ain't got one," Petey said. "Got to go to Star Forks for that."

"No," Clint said, "but you have a vet and a vet can handle a bullet wound as well as a doctor."

"But she's busy with your horse."

"I know," Clint said. He was already wearing his gun so he just grabbed his hat and stepped out into the hall. "Is there a back door here, Petey?"

"Yes, sir."

"Show me," Clint said, and closed the door to his room.

By the time Butler got back to the hotel the other four men were arguing in the lobby about which two were going to have to share a room.

"I ain't sharin'," Tolan said, "not when Hardin gets to stay at the rooming house."

"Hardin's the boss," Butler said, coming up behind them. Of the four men he had been riding with Hardin the longest. "That's why he gets the rooming house."

"Well, I ain't splittin' a room," Tolan said.

"Tell you what," Butler said. "Ben and Will can share a room because they're both wounded and are gonna have to get looked at."

Ben Packer and Will Taylor agreed.

"Let's get it done, then," Butler said. He looked at Ed Powell. "Ed, you and me can take the horses over to the livery."

"Okay."

"Who died and made you boss?" Tolan asked. He was the youngest, and always chafing at the bit.

"I'm just makin' suggestions, Johnny," Butler said, "like suggestin' that you should get your own room."

"Well," Tolan said, "there's a suggestion I like."

"Ed," Butler said, "let's get those horses took care of."

• • •

END OF THE TRAIL

As Clint and Petey entered the livery stable the doctor looked up in annoyance. She was sitting on a bale of hay she had pulled over next to the fallen gelding.

"What the hell—"

"Sorry, Doc," Clint said, "but Petey saw six men ride into town and he seems to think they're hardcases."

"Petey?" she said, looking at the boy.

"Three of 'em are hurt, doc. I'm sure of it."

"They're going to want to put their horses in here," Clint said, "and they'll want a doctor."

"There's no doctor here," she said, firmly.

"No, but there's you," Clint said. "You can remove a bullet, can't you?"

"Well, yes, but—"

"Petey," Clint said, "go and tell your sheriff about the six men."

"I'll tell him," Petey said, "but he ain't gonna do nothin'."

"That's okay," Clint said. "You tell him, anyway."

"Okay."

"What are you going to do?" Abby Fuller asked him.

"Well," he said, "for the time being, I guess I'm going to be the liveryman."

Butler and Powell stopped in front of the livery with the six horses and Butler dismounted.

"Hello the livery!"

The front doors of the livery opened and a man stepped out. He was wearing a gun on his hip and didn't look or stand like any liveryman Butler had ever seen before.

"Can I help you?"

"We need to put our horses up," Butler said. "Got room?"

"Plenty of room," Clint said. "Let me have them and I'll take them inside."

"We can take them in," Powell said.

"Sorry," Clint said. "Vet's inside with a horse that's down. She doesn't want him spooked. I'll take your animals in one at a time. You might as well take your saddlebags or anything else you want now."

Butler looked up at Powell, who nodded and dismounted. Hardin, Packer, Taylor and Johnny Tolan already had their saddlebags and rifles, so Butler and Powell each only had to remove their own.

"How much?" Butler asked.

"Settle up when you leave," Clint said.

The two men exchanged a glance again.

"All right, then..." Butler said, and he and Powell turned and walked away.

Clint waited until they were out of sight, then opened the livery doors wide and walked the horses in one by one. He put them each in a stall, unsaddled them, and rubbed them down while Doc Fuller watched.

"What did you think?" she asked, when he was almost done.

"Once again," Clint said, "I don't think Petey is as dumb as he looks."

"He's not dumb at all," Abby said, "just a little slow."

As if on cue Petey came walking through the door.

"Did you tell the sheriff?" Clint asked.

"I did. He said he couldn't do nothin' unless they was startin' trouble."

"He's part-time," Abby said. "He's not going to look for trouble."

"That's fine," Clint said. "Petey, can you get these horses fed?"

"Sure thing, Mr. Adams."

"There's a man with a bullet in his leg," Clint said, "and one with one in his arm, according to Petey. Can you handle that?"

"I could," she said, "but I'd have to leave Duke."

"We'll figure something out," Clint said.

"What if they recognized you?" she asked.

"I didn't even know that you recognized me," he said.

"Petey told me."

"Ah. Well, if they recognize me I don't think they'll do anything."

"Why not?"

"If they're shot up, like Petey says, chances are they're on the run," Clint explained. "If they're on the run they're not going to want to attract attention."

"I see," she said. "Should I wait until they come looking for me?"

"Probably," Clint said, "just in case Petey's wrong and they don't need doctoring."

"And when they do come looking for me?"

"Send Petey for me," he said. "I'll come and spell you by Duke."

She looked down at the big gelding, whose eyes were closed, and stroked his neck.

"Maybe they'll wait until morning," Clint said. "Maybe they won't. We'll just have to wait and see."

"All right," Abby said.

"Petey, you stay with the doc, okay?" Clint called out.

"Sure thing, Mr. Adams. Anything you say."

Abby smiled and said, "You have a fan."

"I don't need a fan," Clint said, and just when she was thinking the statement might have been harsh he added, "but a new friend is always welcome."

SEVEN

Rebecca Bradford got her new boarder settled into his room and then offered to bring him something to eat.

"That would be very nice of you, Mrs. Bradford," Cord Hardin said, settling himself down onto the bed. As soon as his butt touched the mattress he knew he'd made the right choice.

"What is it?" she asked.

"Oh," he said, "nothing ... I haven't been on a mattress this soft in a long time."

"Well, why don't you get into bed," she said, "and I'll take care of you. I mean, I'll bring you something to eat."

"Thank you."

She hurried from the room before she made a complete fool of herself. This had never happened before, not even with her late husband. She had *never* been this sexually aroused by a man in her life, and it scared her. Her stomach was doing flip flops and she was ... well, she was *wet* between her legs. She would have liked nothing better than to get into bed with this man and take care of him....

Alone in the kitchen, preparing something for Cord Hardin to eat, Rebecca Bradford blushed.

• • •

After Quinn Butler got settled in his room he went down the hall and knocked on Ed Powell's door.

"What'd you think of that liveryman?" he asked.

"That weren't no liveryman, Quinn," Powell said. "You see the way he wore his gun?"

"And the way he watched both of us at the same time," Butler said. "I noticed. We better tell Hardin."

"Right. What about the others?"

"I don't want to tell Johnny Tolan anything," Butler said, "and Ben and Will have to get some rest. 'Sides, we're gonna have to bring them that vet Cord's been talkin' about."

"So just us?"

"Just us."

They left their rooms and walked down the hall to the lobby of the small hotel. Tolan was already there, asking the clerk where he could get something to eat.

"You'd have to go to Mrs. Bradford's rooming house," the clerk said. "South end of town."

Tolan looked at Butler.

"That must be where Hardin is."

"Must be," Butler said. "We was just goin' over there."

"I'll tag along," Tolan said. "Seems that's the only place to get somethin' to eat."

Butler and Powell exchanged a look, and then Butler said, "Come ahead, then."

The three men walked to the south end of town, watched by Clint, who had been approaching the hotel just as they stepped out the front door. He waited until they were out of sight, and then entered.

"How many men checked in?" he asked the clerk.

"Five, in the last three rooms," the man said.

"What about a sixth man? Did you hear anything about him?"

"They said somebody named Cord was staying at Mrs. Bradford's."

"And where are they going now?"

"Over to Mrs. Bradford's to get something to eat, and to talk to the other man."

"They called him Cord?"

"One of them said 'Cord,' " the clerk said, "and then another one said 'Hardin.' "

"Cord Hardin?" Clint asked.

"Yes. Do you know him?"

"No," Clint said, "I don't know him."

Although he didn't know Cord Hardin to look at, Clint knew the name. Hardin claimed to be kin to Wes Hardin—John Wesley Hardin—who Clint *did* know, which was how he knew that this Hardin was not related to Wes. Still, he had heard of the man, and none of it was good. And if he was in town with his whole gang—and some of them shot up—it must have meant they'd just come off a bank job.

"No," Clint said, "I don't know him . . ."

Instead of going to his room Clint left the hotel and crossed over to the general store.

EIGHT

When Clint entered the general store he assumed that the man behind the counter was Ben Pepper, the part-time sheriff.

"Sheriff Pepper?" he asked.

The man stiffened and then stared at Clint for a moment before answering.

"That's more an honorary title than anything else," he said. "Who wants to know?"

"My name's Clint Adams," Clint said. "I sent Petey in a little while ago to tell you about some men who rode into town?"

Pepper relaxed a bit, hearing Clint's name. He was in his early fifties, wearing an apron around some old work clothes. There wasn't a badge or a gun in sight.

"That's right," Pepper said, "Peter was here. I told him I couldn't do nothin' if they weren't breakin' the law."

"Well, they're not, so far," Clint said, "but I found out who they are."

"Oh? Who?"

"Have you ever heard of Cord Hardin?"

The man frowned.

"I heard of John Wesley Hardin," he said. "But no Cord Hardin."

"Well, Cord claims to be related to Wes, but he's not," Clint said. "Still, he is a bank robber, and he is here in town with four members of his gang."

"Bank robbers?" Pepper said. "Whatta we got to worry about? We ain't got no bank."

"I know that," Clint said. "Chances are they're only here to lay low for a while and lick their wounds."

"They're wounded?"

"Some of them, but I don't know how bad."

"We ain't got a doc, either. Why don't they just move on to Star Forks?"

"That'd be too big as place for them," Clint said. "They like this place because it's small, doesn't have much law and you don't have a telegraph."

"First time I heard of somebody comin' here on purpose," Pepper said.

"Well, they're here."

"As long as they don't bother nobody, there's no reason for me to do anythin', right?"

"That's right," Clint said. "I'm just warning you, Sheriff. If they happen to find out who I am, there may be trouble."

"So why don't you leave?"

"I don't have a horse."

"Buy one," Pepper said. "In fact, I'll give you one."

"No, I have one, but he's down, right now," Clint said. "The vet is looking after him. Look, I intend to stay out of their way. I'm just letting you know who they are."

"If you wasn't here," Pepper said, "I wouldn't know who they are, and there'd be no trouble."

"Well," Clint said, "there's not going to be any trouble from me. I just want you to know."

"Fine," Pepper said, "that's just what we want, no trouble."

Clint realized he was wasting his time. Pepper was a shopkeeper, nothing more. The town probably just felt they had to have *somebody* be sheriff, and Pepper got stuck with the job.

"Okay, Mr. Pepper," Clint said, "I'll leave you alone now. Have a good evening."

"I was just about to close up."

Pepper followed Clint to the door and closed up, locking it firmly behind Clint.

It was odd how things happened, him and the Cord Hardin gang ending up here at the same time. Since he wasn't a lawman, though, and they were apparently licking their wounds, maybe there wouldn't be any reason for them to interact, at all.

He went back to the hotel so Petey could find him if Abby Fuller sent for him.

NINE

Butler took Powell and Tolan to Mrs. Bradford's rooming house or boardinghouse or whatever she called it. All he cared about was that it was the house he'd left Hardin off in front of. He knocked on the door while the other two men looked around.

"What a dead place," Tolan said.

"That's why we're here," Butler said.

The door opened and a woman appeared.

"Hey," Tolan said to Powell, "this place might not be so bad. A little old for me, but still not bad."

"Quiet," Powell said.

"Hello, Ma'am," Butler said.

"Can I help you?"

"We're looking for our friend, Cord Hardin."

"Yes, Mr. Hardin is here, but he's in bed now."

"Ma'am, we really have to talk to him. See, he's our boss and we all rode in together."

"I see," she said. "Well, I suppose you had better come in, then. I'll show you to his room."

All three men entered the house and followed her up the stairs to the second floor.

"I told you this place would be better than the hotel," Tolan hissed at Powell.

They went down a hall to a room and waited while Mrs. Bradford knocked on the door.

"Come in." Butler recognized Hardin's voice.

"There are some men here who say they're friends of yours," she said to him.

"Let them in, Rebecca," he said. "It's all right."

She stepped away from the door and said, "You can go in."

"Ma'am," Butler said, "would it be possible for us to get something to eat while we're here?"

"I'll have something ready when you come down."

She started down the hall but Tolan was in her way. He smiled at her, but didn't move.

"Would you ask your little brother to move out of my way?" she said to either of them.

"Move, Johnny," Powell said. "Let the lady by."

Tolan moved, but grudgingly, and then watched Rebecca Bradford walk down the hall.

"Yessir," he said, "not bad," and then followed Butler and Powell into the room.

Hardin was lying in a bed that had the thickest mattress Johnny Tolan had ever seen.

"That's it," he said. "I'm moving' over here."

The other three men ignored him.

"You look comfortable," Butler said. "How's the side?"

"Better, now that the horse isn't jarring me every minute. You boys get settled at the hotel?"

"Ain't much of a hotel," Tolan complained. "No food."

Hardin looked at Butler.

"We can eat here," Butler said. "The desk clerk told us Mrs. Bradford'll feed us even if we're not guests."

"Sure," Tolan said, "as long as we pay."

"Cord, we need to get Packer and Taylor looked at."

"The vet," Hardin said. "Her name's Fuller, Abigail Fuller. Find her, tell her you're with me. She'll take care of them."

"The vet," Butler repeated. "She's in the livery."

"How do you know that?"

"Feller told us," Powell said.

"What feller?"

"A man who's no liveryman," Butler said. "Wears a gun like he knows how to use it. Wouldn't let us in the livery 'cause the vet was in there with a fallen horse."

"What happened to the horses?" Hardin asked.

"He took them in."

"Well, get over to the livery and tell her to look at Ben and Will," Hardin said. "Two men are more important than a horse."

"What about the feller?" Powell asked.

"Who is he?"

"Don't know."

"Well, find out," Hardin said, shifting in the bed. He hadn't been in it long and already his butt was starting to hurt. A mattress this soft might not have been such a good idea, after all. "I don't want no surprises in this town."

"Okay," Butler said.

"How about local law?" Hardin asked. "Is there any?"

"We ain't found out, yet," Butler said.

"Well, go and do it," Hardin said. "Find out who this feller is, and who the law is."

"We gotta eat," Tolan said. "The woman's fixin' somethin'—"

"Eat when you're done," Hardin said, "and take it over to the hotel. Take some for Packer and Taylor, too. She'll keep it warm for you until you get back."

"All right, Cord," Butler said.

"But we gotta—" Tolan started, but Butler turned and

started for the door. Tolan had to move, too, or be knocked over.

"Hey—" he said, out in the hall.

"You heard Cord," Butler said. "Let's go."

TEN

It was getting dark but Petey was able to see the three men walking toward the livery.

"Three men comin', Doc," he said to Abby Fuller.

She came to the door and looked out. The men were wearing guns and walking with purposeful strides.

"Go out the back, Petey, and get Mr. Adams."

"Yes, Ma'am," he said. "He'll take care of all three of them."

She grabbed him and turned him around.

"Understand what I'm saying to you, Petey," she said. "I don't want Mr. Adams to come rushing over here to save me. I just want him to come and stay with the horse while I'm gone. Understand?"

"Sure, Doc, sure," the boy said, "I understand."

"Then go," she said, releasing him.

Petey turned to leave and said, "He's the Gunsmith. He can take care of all three of them."

He was gone before Abby could say anything else to him.

When the three men entered the livery they swung the doors wide open so that whatever light was left came streaming in. Still, it was hard for them to see until their eyes adjusted to the dimmer light of the interior of the stable. What they saw was a woman leaning over a big black horse that was lying on the ground. She was rubbing its neck. Tolan thought that this woman—although also too old for him—was better-looking than the one at the rooming house.

"Ma'am," Butler said, "are you the vet?"

"That's right."

Tolan walked to her, grabbed her by the arm, pulled her to her feet and said, "Come with us."

"I beg your pardon," she said, pulling her arm away. "I don't appreciate being manhandled."

"You're comin' with us—"

"Johnny!" Butler said.

Tolan turned and glared at Butler. He knew that Butler had ridden with Hardin the longest, but when he looked at the man he saw someone pushing fifty, grey in his hair, thick through the arms, shoulders and chest but also growing thick in the middle. Hardin and Butler were both past their prime.

"Ma'am," Butler said, "I'm sorry he grabbed you like that. That's a right fine looking animal. Too bad he's ailin'."

"Yes, it is too bad," she said, rubbing her arm where Tolan had grabbed her.

"Is he gonna be all right?"

"He should be, but I have to stay with him until—"

"Ma'am, we got two men shot and no doctor in town. I'm afraid we're gonna have to ask you to come with us."

"How badly hurt are they?"

"One's got a through hole in his arm," Powell said, "the other one still has a bullet in his leg. It's gotta come out."

"Yes, you're right," she said, "it does, but . . . I'm a vet, not a doctor. One of you could probably—"

"Ma'am," Butler said, "we ride with Cord Hardin."

Abby froze at the sound of the name.

"You know him?" Tolan asked. "Know who he is?"

"I know who he is," she said, "and I know him—or I knew him, a long time ago. Is—is he here?"

"Yes, Ma'am," Butler said.

"Where?"

"The rooming house."

"He's hurt, too," Powell said, "but not shot."

"What's wrong with him?"

"Got thrown from his horse," Butler said. "Might have a busted rib or two."

"Not much I can do about that."

"We know that, Ma'am," Butler said, "that's why we want you to look at the two men who were shot."

Abby Fuller had not yet recovered from hearing Cord Hardin's name. She didn't think she'd ever hear it again, especially not living here, in Firecreek.

"Oh, come on," Tolan said, "let's just take her—"

"Johnny," Butler said, "don't put your hands on the woman again."

Tolan stiffened, then turned to face Butler.

"How many?" Clint asked Petey as he followed him out of the hotel.

"Three of them," Petey said, "and mean lookin'."

"They probably just want her to look at their wounded."

"She said she didn't want you savin' her," Petey said, "she just wanted you to stay with the horse."

"As long as they need her," Clint said, "they won't hurt her."

They were approaching the livery when they heard the shot. Clint broke into a run, outdistancing Petey and beating him to the stable. As he entered, gun in hand, Abby and another man were crouched by a man who had been shot in the left shoulder. The third man—the youngest—was just holstering his weapon.

"Well, Doc," he said, "looks like you got a third man to look after."

Tolan walked out past Clint and said, "You missed all the excitement, friend."

Clint let him go, because nobody was saying not to. Apparently, there had been a falling out amongst the thieves.

"He's crazy, Quinn," Powell said to Butler. "I didn't think he'd draw."

"We have to get him to the hotel," Abby said to Powell. She looked at Clint. "Stay with Duke."

"Do you need help—"

"This man and I can handle it," she said. "Stay with your horse."

Clint nodded and watched as Abby and the other man helped the man he heard called "Quinn" out of the livery and past Petey.

"You want me to go, too, Mr. Adams?"

"Yes, Petey," Clint said. "Just stay in the hotel lobby and wait for her. Call me if there's any more trouble."

"Okay."

Petey ran after the others and Clint turned to look at Duke. The big gelding acted as if he hadn't even heard the shot.

ELEVEN

Abby and Ed Powell got Quinn Butler to his room and onto his bed, and then she sent Powell for some water and bandages. She also needed some instruments with which to remove the bullet. She assumed Petey was in the lobby, and told Powell to send Petey for them. Finally, she got the bullet out of Butler's shoulders and bandaged it up.

"I don't understand," she said, while she was working. "Why would your own friend shoot you?"

"We ain't friends," Butler said, flexing his hand to make sure it worked, "we just ride together—and we ain't gonna be doing that too much longer after Cord finds out what Tolan did."

"What will Cord do?" she asked.

"He'll kill him."

She sat back and surveyed her work.

"I saw that man Tolan draw," she said. "He's very fast."

"Yeah, he is," Butler said. "Faster than I thought."

"Me, too," Powell said. "You think Cord can take him, Quinn?"

"Cord can take anybody, Ed."

"Even the Gunsmith?"

Butler looked at Powell.

"Why'd you ask me that?"

"I checked the register while I was out in the lobby," Powell said. "That feller at the livery signed in as Clint Adams."

Butler looked at Abby.

"Is that right?" he asked. "Is he the Gunsmith?"

"Yes, he is," she said. "That's his horse I'm working on in the livery. That's the only reason he's here."

"When did he—"

She stood up abruptly and said, "If you want me to take care of your other friends you better take me to them. I have to get back to that horse, or he won't make it through the night."

"The horse is hurt that bad?" Butler asked.

"He's ill," Abby said, "very ill."

Butler frowned. He'd heard stories about the Gunsmith and his big black gelding. A horse like that was special.

"Take her to Ben and Will, Ed," he said, "and then let her go back to the horse."

"What about Tolan?"

"Do we know where he is?"

"No."

"Forget about him," Butler said. "Get the boys taken care of first, and then you can go and talk to Cord about Tolan, and about Adams."

"And the lawman," Powell said. "We got to find out about him, too."

"I'm sure the doc, here, knows all about the local law."

"He's part-time," she said, "just a storekeeper."

"Why are you so free with that information?" Powell asked.

"Because there's nothing in this town for you and your friends to steal," she said. "Come on, take me to those other two men."

END OF THE TRAIL

• • •

Clint sat on the bale of hay next to Duke and stared down at his proud gelding. They had been through a lot together, and if Duke got through this Clint swore he'd take better care of him. He could take him back to Labyrinth and let him live out his days there in peace. They had been all over the West together, but it was finally time for Duke to stay in one place.

He also decided that he *wasn't* ready to be put out to pasture. He still had some travelling in him, and all he needed to do was find the right horse to do it with. It was going to be hard, because he was used to Duke. He didn't know where he was going to find a horse that would live up to the big gelding. There was one, up in Montana, that he had used a time or two, but it didn't belong to him and he had no intentions of trying to claim it. Besides, that horse was white, and he wanted something else. Maybe not another black one, but he thought that riding around on a white horse would make him an even bigger target.

Duke's breathing was smooth for the moment, but Clint watched carefully for any sign of change and hoped that Abby Fuller would get back before something went wrong.

Abby dropped the bullet into the basin and said to Will Taylor, "You should be all right, now."

"Thanks, Doc."

She bandaged the leg, then went and looked at Ben Packer's wound. The bullet had gone right through his arm, and there was no sign of infection. She cleaned it thoroughly to keep it that way, and then bandaged him up, as well.

Packer flexed his arm and said, "For a vet you're a pretty good doctor, Ma'am."

"Thank you," she said, standing up. She turned to look at Ed Powell. "I've got to get back to the livery."

"All right, Ma'am," he said. "I don't see why not. Is there anything you'd like me to tell Cord for you?"

She stared at Powell for a few moments, things she wished she'd said to Cord Hardin years ago tumbling about in her head, but finally just shook her head and said, "No, nothing."

"All right, then," Powell said. "You can go, Ma'am . . . and thanks."

She left without saying another word.

TWELVE

After Abby Fuller left the hotel Ed Powell went back to the rooming house to tell Cord Hardin everything that had happened. When Mrs. Bradford answered the door she was in a robe, and had an annoyed look on her face.

"It's about time," she said. "I can't keep this food out all night, you know."

"Sorry, Ma'am," Powell said. "I'll take it with me when I leave—after I talk to Mr. Hardin again."

"Go on up," she said, with a sigh. "I'll get the food ready."

What Powell didn't know was that when he knocked he caught Rebecca Bradford standing in front of the mirror in her room—naked. She had been inspecting her body, wondering if a man—specifically, Cord Hardin—would still find her desirable. She had been cupping both of her big breasts in her hands, thinking that they didn't look so bad, when Powell knocked. She'd hurriedly tossed on the robe and answered the door.

Now she went into the kitchen to pack up the food for Powell and the other men.

• • •

"Come on in, Ed," Hardin said.

Powell had expected to find Hardin still in bed but the man was standing at the window. "I saw you come walking up. What's going on? I thought I might have heard a shot before, but I couldn't be sure."

"That was at the livery," Powell said. "You heard it all the way over here?"

"What happened?"

Powell hesitated, then said, "Johnny shot Butler."

Hardin stiffened.

"Is Quinn dead?"

"No," Powell said, "Johnny hit him in the left arm."

"What happened?"

"He outdrew Quinn."

"I mean, *what* happened?" Hardin said, again. "Why did it happen?"

"Oh . . . well, Johnny was manhandling the doc and Quinn tried to get him to stop."

"What did he do to her?"

"Just grabbed her arm. Quinn wanted her treated with more respect—you know, like a lady."

"That's because she *is* a lady," Hardin said. "Where's Quinn?"

"In his room. She dug the bullet out and bandaged him, then took care of Ben and Will. She did real good, Cord, like she was a real doc."

"That's because she was, once," Hardin said, "when I knew her."

"When was that?"

"A long time ago." Hardin looked Powell. "How does she look, Ed?"

"Good," Powell said, "she looks good, Cord. Real pretty. Blonde hair, sturdy body—almost like the lady downstairs, but maybe some prettier."

"She was always a pretty woman," Hardin said. "Where's Tolan?"

"Don't know."

"This isn't much of a town, Ed," Hardin said. "Find him, tell him I want to see him."

"Cord . . ."

"What?"

"He's fast," Powell said. "That kid's fast. I didn't know he was that fast!"

"I did."

"Can you take him?"

"That might not be necessary."

"But . . . he shot Quinn."

"And he'll answer to me for it," Hardin said. "Just find him and tell him to come here."

"What if . . ."

"What if what?"

"What if he don't want to?" Powell asked. "What if he shoots me on sight?"

"Take off your gun," Hardin said. "If you're not wearin' it when you find him, he won't shoot you."

"O-okay."

"What about that other feller?" Hardin asked. "The one at the livery? Did you find out who he is?"

"Oh yeah," Powell said, "I found out."

Hardin waited, his back to Powell, still looking out the window.

"Well? Are you gonna tell me?"

"He's Clint Adams, Cord."

Hardin remained silent for a few moments, then asked, "Are you sure?"

"Yep."

"Clint Adams, the Gunsmith?"

"Yes."

"How can you be sure?"

"The doc told me so," Powell said.

"What's he doin' here?"

"She's takin' care of his horse," Powell said, even though the question wasn't directed at him. "She says his horse is real sick."

Hardin hesitated, then said, "That could explain it."

Powell waited. Hardin finally turned and faced him.

"When you find Johnny, tell him Clint Adams is in town."

"Tell Johnny?" Powell asked. "If I do that, Cord, you know he'll go after him."

"That's right, Ed," Hardin said. "I do know. Tell him."

THIRTEEN

Clint looked up as Abby Fuller entered the livery. He'd found a single storm lamp in the stable and had lit it. She looked very lovely bathed in its yellow light, her face touched with concern for Duke.

"How is he?" she asked.

"He's been resting comfortably since you left."

"Good."

She crouched down next to Clint, putting one hand on his leg to keep him from getting up.

"Stay a few minutes," she said. "we have to talk."

"About what happened earlier?"

"About that, and more."

"All right."

She remained silent.

"Whenever you're ready."

"I'm composing my thoughts."

"Why don't you tell me what you were doing while you were away?" he asked.

"I patched up three men," she said. "The one who was shot here, and two other who had already been shot."

"Cord Hardin's gang."

She turned her head quickly and looked at him.

"You know about Cord?"

"I know about him, yes," he said. "Why do I get the feeling that you actually *know* him?"

She looked away.

"Because I do know him—at least, I did . . . once."

"When?"

"A long time ago."

"Where?"

She hesitated, then said, "Where doesn't matter." She started stroking Duke's neck. "When, where, what we were doing, none of that matters."

"What does matter, Abby?"

"That he's here, with his men," she said. "That we're in danger—those of us who live here, that is. Not you."

"Why not me?"

"Because you're like—" she started, then stopped abruptly.

"Because I'm like them?" Clint asked. "Is that what you were going to say?"

"I have no right to judge you," she said. "I'm just worried about . . . this town."

"Why?" he asked. "Why are you worried about this town? What are you doing in a place like Firecreek?"

"It's my safe haven."

"From what?"

She didn't answer."

"From Hardin?"

She hesitated, then said, "Among other things."

"Like what?"

"The past," she said. "Just the past."

"Did you see Hardin tonight?"

"No," she said, "but they said he was hurt. Maybe some broken ribs."

"Will you be seeing him?"

"I . . . don't know."

"What do you want me to do?"

"Keep us safe."

"I have nothing against these six men, Abby."

She looked at him then and said, "But you owe me."

"Oh," he said, "I see."

"That's my bill, Clint," she said. "Keep us all safe, until they leave. You know what happened here. One of them lost his head and shot the other one. They ride together, and he shot him. What would he do to one of us if he got angry enough?"

"Probably worse."

"Right," she said. "And the sheriff we have will be useless—less than useless."

He studied her face until she turned it away. Her hand continued to stroke Duke's neck.

"All right, Abby," he said. "If that's the price for Duke's life, then I'll pay it."

"That's the price," she said. "You have to stay anyway until Duke is well enough to travel."

"Do you think they'll be ready to travel before Duke?"

"I think so," she said. "Two or three days, maybe."

"Even the gunshot wounds will be ready to move then," Clint said, "but what about Hardin's ribs?" Some wounds were even worse than getting shot, he thought. Ribs took a while to heal when they were cracked.

"Maybe they're not cracked," she said.

"You won't know that without seeing him."

"I know."

"Will you go to him?"

"No," she said, "but he'll send for me."

"And you'll wait for that?"

"Yes."

He sighed and stood up.

"Probably not tonight, though."

"No."

"Then I'm going to get some sleep," he said. "It'll be tiring work keeping even a town this small safe."

FOURTEEN

Quite by accident Johnny Tolan managed to find a place where he could get a drink. At the north end of town, about a hundred yards from the livery, he found a small, one-table saloon and trading post that stayed open late.

Tolan nursed a beer at that one table while also nursing a little bit of guilt at having shot Quinn Butler. He felt guilty because the man he wanted to shoot was Cord Hardin. He thought that by shooting Hardin he'd be able to take over the gang. Shooting Butler wasn't going to accomplish anything but make it hard to get Butler to follow him, in the end.

Maybe, he thought, he should apologize.

Ed Powell managed to find Tolan by asking the desk clerk at the hotel where somebody could get a drink. The clerk sent him to the place Tolan had already found on his own.

When Powell entered Tolan looked up at him.

"Get a beer," Tolan called out, "on me."

Powell went to the bar, got a beer and joined Tolan at the single table. Other than the bartender—a bored-looking man in his sixties—they were the only two people in the place. That was good, because one more person would have made the place crowded.

"How's Quinn?" Tolan asked.

"He'll be okay," Powell said. "The doc got the bullet out."

"She see to Ben and Will?'

"Yep," Powell said, "they'll be fine, too."

"That's good," Tolan said, "that's real good. I'm really sorry for shooting Butler, Ed. I just . . . he pushed me, ya know?"

"Don't tell me," Powell said, "tell him."

"I will," Tolan said, "I swear I will. In the morning, when we all get up, I'll tell him."

"Good," Powell said, "that's good."

There was a moment of silence and then Tolan asked, "Did you tell Hardin what happened?"

"I did."

"What'd he say?"

"He wants to see you."

"Tonight?"

"Tomorrow would probably do."

"Okay," Tolan said, nodding, "I'll go and see him tomorrow."

"There's one more thing you ought to know, Johnny."

"What's that?"

"That feller we saw at the livery?"

"The one don't look like a liveryman?"

"That's him," Powell said. "We found out who he is."

"Oh? Who?"

"His name's Clint Adams."

Tolan's arm stopped with his beer mug halfway to his mouth. Suddenly, his eyes were shining. He licked his lips and set the beer mug down carefully on the table.

"The Gunsmith?"

"That's him."

Tolan was silent for a moment, then he said, "Honest to God, Ed? The *Gunsmith*?"

"It was him," Powell said.

"How do you know?"

"I saw his name in the register."

"Could be a coincidence."

"The doctor said it was him," Powell said. "That's his horse she's takin' care of."

"Jesus Christ," Tolan said. "What luck. What *crazy* luck, to ride into a nothin' town like this and find the Gunsmith waiting here. It's like findin' a gold mine."

"I guess, if you want to look at it that way."

"Does Hardin know?"

"He does."

"Is he gonna go after him?"

"Not with his ribs hurtin' the way they are."

"Who else would do it?"

"I don't know, Johnny," Powell said. "Ben, Will and Quinn are all in no shape for it. Besides, none of them are gunhands."

"What about you?"

"Me?" Powell asked. "Go against the Gunsmith? Not a chance."

"Well," Tolan said, "I guess that leaves it to me, then, doesn't it?"

"Why does somebody have to go after him?" Powell asked.

"Whataya mean?" Tolan asked. "He's the Gunsmith. *Somebody's* gotta try him, for Chrissake."

"Well," Powell said, "it ain't gonna be me."

"It's gonna be me, then," Johnny Tolan said. "It's gonna be me. And I ain't only gonna try him, Ed. I'll gonna *kill* 'im."

"Are you that good, Johnny?"

"You saw my move today," Tolan said. "What do you think?"

"It was fast," Powell said, "fastest I ever saw."

"Well, there ya go," Tolan said. "You saw it with your own eyes." He picked up his beer mug and smiled at Powell over it. "I'm gonna kill me the Gunsmith. Hot damn!"

FIFTEEN

"Why aren't you in bed?"

Cord Hardin turned and saw Rebecca Bradford standing in the doorway. She was wearing a robe. As a man who had been with a lot of women over the years Hardin had been reading her signals all day. Looking at her now, he knew she was naked under the robe.

He stepped away from the window.

"I can't sleep," he said. "Too many nights on the cold ground, I guess. I'm not used to plush mattresses."

"Maybe," she said, "you just don't like being in the bed alone."

Hardin decided not to play games with her. She'd been sending him signals all day and now that he had been thinking about Abby Fuller for the past few hours he was beyond playing games.

He walked to her, grabbed her by the front of the robe and pulled her roughly into the room.

"Wha—" she said.

"Is this what you want?" he asked.

"But—"

He kissed her, a hard brutal kiss that would leave her lips feeling bruised, but on fire. As he kissed her he slid his hand inside her robe, cupped one full, firm breast and squeezed it. He could feel the hardness of the nipple right in the center of his palm.

With his other hand he pulled the belt on the robe so that it opened, then used both hands to let it drop to the floor. Once she was naked he stepped back to look at her.

She was lovely, full and womanly, with heavy breasts, wide hips, a soft belly with a deep belly button, fleshy thighs . . . and he knew when he turned her around she'd have a fine, wide ass.

"This is what you want, isn't it?" he asked.

Before she could answer he shucked his shirt and dropped his underwear to the floor. Her eyes went right to his rigid penis, red and pulsing, long and hard. She licked her lips and moved toward him, reaching out and taking the hot, hard column of flesh into both hands.

"Your ribs," she said, in a low, hungry voice, "you must let me do everything."

That hadn't been his plan. His plan had been to take her hard, and in several different ways. First, he was going to throw her onto the bed on her back and take her that way. Then he was going to slide out of her, raise her legs very high and take her that way, in the back. But he knew now that each thrust of his hips, whether he was in her puss or her behind, would cause pain to lance through his side.

"Yes," he said, "all right."

He started for the bed but she would not release her hold on him.

"No," she said, "not here. My bed, down the hall."

"Lead the way."

She did, keeping his penis in her hand the whole way so he could not escape her. She tugged him into her room, laid him out on the bed and began to work on him with her mouth and tongue. Eventually she nestled down between his legs and licked the length of his penis like a kid with a licorice stick. In the end she climbed up on him, supported her weight with her own legs and lowered herself onto his penis. He slid into her wetness with ease and she rode him up and down, taking all her weight on her arms and legs so as not to hurt his ribs. Right at the end, though, when he reared up and exploded into her the pleasure mixed with the pain and as he cried out became became indistinguishable from one another . . .

"Are you all right?" she asked, moments later.

"I'm fine."

"Me, too," she said, lying beside him.

"And you know something?" he asked.

"What?"

"Your mattress is better than mine."

"If you like it so much," she said, "you can use it the rest of the time you're here."

"Thank you."

"But you'll have to take me with it."

"I think," he said, "I can handle that."

Ed Powell managed to get Johnny Tolan back to his room. He dumped the younger man on his hotel bed, fully dressed, and removed his gunbelt so he wouldn't roll over and shoot himself. Just for a moment he considered shooting the man himself, while he was asleep. It would probably save a lot of trouble later on. In the end he simply hung the gunbelt on the bedpost and left the room. Before going to his own he went to Quinn Butler's, knocked and entered.

"How're you doin'?"

"I'm okay," Quinn said. "That vet did a good job. Did you talk to Hardin?"

"I did. He wants to see Johnny tomorrow. He wasn't near as mad as I thought he'd be."

"The funny thing is," Butler said, "neither am I."

"Why not?"

"I don't think Johnny can help it, sometimes," Butler said. "I saw his eyes just before he drew. I don't think he knew what he was doing."

"You got a lot more forgiveness in you than I do," Powell said, "but just for your information, I found Johnny and he says he's gonna apologize to you tomorrow."

"That's fine," Butler said. "Don't get me wrong, though. I still don't think he belongs in the gang."

"Neither do I," Powell said, "but I guess that'll depend on what Cord thinks, huh?"

"Yeah."

"You know," Powell said, "Clint Adams is in the other room, here. Right down the hall."

"I know." Butler's eyes widened. "Did you tell Johnny that Adams was in town?"

"I did."

"Why'd you do that?"

"Cord told me to."

"That sonofagun," Butler said, cradling his left arm. "He's gonna let Johnny go after Adams, and let Adams take care of the problem for us."

"Yeah, but I saw Johnny's move in the livery, Quinn," Powell said. "What if Johnny does manage to kill Adams?"

"Well," Butler said, "if he does that, he'll be the man who killed the Gunsmith, right?"

"Right."

"So why would he want to ride around with a bunch of bank robbers like us after that?"

Powell smiled and said, "You got a point."

SIXTEEN

Clint did not sleep well that night. He was worried about Duke, knew that Cord Hardin was somewhere in town, knew that his men were also in the hotel and at least one of them was trigger happy, and he was also worried about Abby Fuller. Could it be a coincidence that the Hardin gang came to this town to recuperate, the same town where she was living? He wondered, too, exactly what her history was with Hardin.

Maybe in the morning he'd ask her to confirm that Cord was not related to Wes.

Abby Fuller dozed on and off while keeping a watchful eye on Duke. The big gelding was doing better than she had anticipated, which meant she was a better vet than even she thought. She had to admit she much preferred working on animals over working on people. They complained less. She also found that being a female vet was much less stressful than trying to be a female doctor, in the West.

She wondered what was going to happen come morning. Would Cord Hardin send for her? Would Clint Adams be able to keep his word and keep the town of Firecreek safe from Hardin and his men? Would Hardin and his gang be ready to travel before Duke was?

She knew one thing. Come morning she was going to need a decent meal, and the only place to get one was at Rebecca Bradford's—where Cord Hardin was staying.

Hardin laid awake for a while after Rebecca fell asleep. She was a lot of woman, Rebecca Bradford. Had probably been hidden away here without a man for quite a while, and he was the lucky recipient of all that pent-up passion, but he still couldn't help thinking about Abby Fuller. It had been over ten years since he'd seen her last. He wondered if her beauty had matured over the years, remembering that Ed Powell said she looked better than Rebecca Bradford. She'd want nothing to do with him, of course, but then all he wanted from her was to fix up his men so they could ride.

Maybe, in the morning, he'd have Ed Powell bring her over to have a look at him—and then he could have a look at her, at the same time.

Rebecca Bradford listened to the sound of Cord Hardin's heartbeat and knew he wasn't asleep. She continued to pretend that she was, and wondered what he was thinking. Of course, the possibility that he might stay in Firecreek with her was ridiculous, but she wondered how long it would take for him and his men to heal enough to leave. He had awakened something in her that she had thought was long dead, and she supposed she'd have to thank him for that, but what was she going to do once he was gone? There wasn't a man worth a damn in Firecreek, and this is where she was stuck. She was just going to have to make the most of having him here for a few days, and hope against hope that he might fall in love with her and want to stay.

Right.
In Firecreek.

Petey Roberts was too excited to sleep. From his regular place in the hayloft he looked down at Doc Fuller and the big black gelding. Having the Gunsmith in town was the most exciting thing that had ever happened in his life, and now that these other men were here, too . . . well, he was just too excited to sleep, wondering what would happen next.

SEVENTEEN

Clint woke in the morning with a bad feeling. He dressed quickly and almost ran to the livery. When he entered Abby turned and looked at him and smiled. Just behind her was Duke, and he was standing up.

"He's all right?"

"The growth has shrunk, and will probably continue to until he can breathe normally. That might not be for a couple of days, though. But he's up, and that's more than encouraging."

"Encouraging?" Clint repeated. "It's wonderful. I could kiss you, Abby!"

She regarded him quizzically and asked, "Why do I think that's not something I'd regret?"

They stood there awkwardly for a moment, and then Clint walked to Duke, who nudged him with his nose.

"How you doing, boy?" he asked. "This lady is some great vet, huh? Pulled you through, didn't she?"

He patted the big gelding's neck while Duke managed to look totally unconcerned.

Clint turned to Abby and said, "You probably need some rest and a good breakfast."

"I can get some rest at home," she said. "For a good breakfast we'd have to go to Mrs. Bradford's rooming house."

"Is that where Hardin is staying?"

"Yes."

"Well," he said, turning to her, "I'm pretty hungry. I'm game if you are."

She smiled and said, "Sure, why not? Got to get it over with sometime, don't I? I might as well have company."

"Can we leave Duke alone?"

"I think he'll be fine. Besides, Petey's up in the hayloft and he's probably watching us right now... aren't you, Petey?"

"Yes, Ma'am."

"You keep an eye on Mr. Adams's horse, you hear?"

"Yes, Ma'am."

"I'll be back later. I'll bring you some breakfast from Mrs. Bradford's, okay?"

"Yes, *Ma'am!*"

Clint and Abby left and started walking to the other end of town—which was no long walk.

"Tell me about this town," he said. "What else is here?"

"General Store you know about, the hotel, the livery, hmm, we've got a small saloon and trading post, the rooming house, a small church—"

"I didn't see a church."

"It's not a real church, it's just a building we use as a church."

"Do you have a minister?"

"A travelling minister," she said. "He comes in about once a month on his way to Star Forks."

"Why do you live here instead of there?" Clint asked. "Or another larger town, somewhere?"

"Truthfully?"

"Truthfully."

"I'm hiding out."

"From what?"

"My past."

"A past that includes Cord Hardin?"

"Among other things."

"Okay," Clint said, "I'm getting too pushy. Tell me about Petey. Where's he from?"

"Around here," she said. "His mother and father had a small farm near here, but they died when he was young. The town sort of adopted him, from what I understand. I've only been here ten years, and he was already here when I arrived. He was doing odd jobs back then, but over the past couple of years he just works at the livery."

"Who owns the livery?"

"The town."

"Is there a town council?"

"Of sorts," she said. "It includes me, Ben Pepper—our part-time sheriff, who you've met—and a few others."

"What about Mrs. Bradford?"

"Her first name's Rebecca," she answered. "She was also here when I got here. Seems her husband died and left her that house and nothing else. She turned it into a rooming house, but since she never has many boarders she's become more a café than anything else. Not that any of us mind. She's the best cook in town, by far."

They were approaching the Bradford house now.

"In the ten years that you've been here has there ever been any trouble, Abby?"

"None."

"That was a quick answer."

"You're wondering how much help Ben Pepper will be if the Hardin gang causes trouble."

"That's what I was wondering."

"I would say none," she answered, "but there's really nothing for me to base that on. I'm afraid you're just going to have to wait and see."

"That's what I thought you'd say."

EIGHTEEN

Rebecca Bradford greeted them very graciously, which immediately made Abby suspicious. She seated them in her dining room and went into the kitchen to prepare breakfast.

"Something's wrong," Abby said.

"Why?"

"She's never this friendly."

"Are the two of you—"

"No, no," Abby said, "we're friends, but she's *never* this gracious, especially not at this time of the morning."

"What could make that kind of change occur?" he asked.

"Only one thing."

"What's that?"

"A man?"

They both looked up at the ceiling.

"Hardin?" he asked.

"He was very charming when I knew him," she said.

"And good-looking?"

"No," she said, "but attractive to women—sort of the way you are."

He smiled.

"What a left-handed way of telling me I'm not good-looking."

"Good-looking men are a dime a dozen," she said.

"Well then, I'll take it as a compliment."

Rebecca Bradford came back into the room with two cups and a pot of coffee. The smells coming from the kitchen were delicious.

"I hear you have a boarder, Rebecca," Abby said.

"Yes."

"Will he be coming down for breakfast?"

"No," she said, "he's recovering from a fall from his horse. Might even have cracked ribs." Rebecca looked at Abby. "Maybe you'd take a look at him, Abby?"

Abby looked at Clint, who shrugged. It was up to her, and suddenly she thought that this would give her the advantage. He certainly wasn't expecting her to walk in on him.

"I can do that now, if you like."

"Would you?" Rebecca said. "Go on up, then."

Abby stood up and started for the stairs.

"What room is he in, Bec?"

"Oh, uh, he's in my room."

"Oh."

"The, uh, other mattresses were too soft for him."

"Uh-huh," Abby said. She looked at Clint. "I'll be back shortly."

He nodded and picked up his coffee.

Abby made her way down the hall to Rebecca's room. It hadn't taken Cord Hardin long to win her over. Apparently, he hadn't changed all that much in ten years.

When she got to the door she knocked and stood in the open doorway until he turned his head to look at her. Their eyes locked and it was as if everything in the world stopped. They just stared at each other for a few moments, each thinking how the other had aged, but certainly with no detriment. She thought he was as attractive as ever, perhaps moreso with the age lines in his face, and he thought that she had become beautiful in her maturity.

"Well," he said.

"Cord."

"You look great."

"Why'd you come here?"

"To see you."

She shook her head.

"No."

"I knew you'd take care of me and my men."

"How did you know?"

He smiled and shrugged.

"How did you know where I was?"

"I found out a long time ago."

"Then why wait until now to come?"

"We were in the area. I understand you took care of my men. Thanks for that."

"I don't appreciate this, Cord. I'm not a doctor here, I'm a vet. I treat animals, not horses—although . . ."

"Now, now," he said, "let's don't get insulting. My men aren't animals."

"Really?" she asked. "I watched one of them shoot another yesterday. Don't animals attack their own kind?"

She was still standing in the doorway, and had no desire to get any closer to him.

"Rebecca Bradford is my friend, Cord."

"So?"

"That's her bed."

"Jealous?"

"Hardly," she said. "I don't want you to hurt her."

"I don't think she's hurting, Abby," he said, "but you could ask her."

"Just get healed and leave town, Cord," she replied. "That would be best for all of us."

"Maybe you can help me heal, Abby?"

She shook her head, said, "There's nothing I can do for cracked ribs," turned, and went back downstairs.

NINETEEN

When Abby came back downstairs her face was stoic. She did not look at Clint. She sat opposite him and remained silent until Rebecca Bradford came back into the room.

"That was quick," Rebecca said. "How is he?"

"Like you said," Abby answered. "Cracked ribs. Not much you can do for that but keep him still."

Abby read perfectly the smile that came to Rebecca's face.

"Oh, Rebecca . . ." she said.

Rebecca misread her friend's remark and smiled all the more.

"Breakfast coming out," she said.

"I take it the reunion did not go well?"

"He hasn't changed."

"Which means?"

She stared at him a moment, then said, "Oh, not that I'm still attracted to him. What I mean is, he's going to hurt her."

"Like he hurt you?"

"Yes."

"Will she listen to you?"

"No," Abby said. "She's been widowed and without a man for a long time . . . but I'll have to try."

Rebecca came out with two plates of ham and eggs, and a basket of fresh biscuits.

"Eat and enjoy," she said. "I have to take something up to Cord."

"Would you do me a favor, Rebecca?" Clint asked.

"If I can."

"Would you tell Cord I'm down here with Abby?"

"Uh, well sure . . . by name?"

"Yes," Clint said. "Clint Adams." In case she had forgotten.

"All right. I'll take his plate up the back steps. I'll be back shortly, in case you need anything else."

"Why did you do that?" Abby asked.

"Same reason you went up," Clint said. "It was going to happen, anyway."

"You think he'll ask to see you?"

"I'm sure he will," Clint said, "but probably not until after breakfast."

"I'm glad my friend checked your ribs," Rebecca said, as she set Hardin's tray in front of him.

"Is that what she said she did?"

"Well, yes . . . didn't she?"

"Oh, sure, sure," Hardin said. "She checked them. Said she couldn't do much about it, though."

"She has someone downstairs with her."

"Oh? Who?"

"A man named Clint Adams."

That arrested the movement of Hardin's fork to his mouth for a moment, and then he completed it.

"Really?"

"Yes. Do you know him?"

"I know of him. He's a very famous man."

"Really?" She frowned.

"They call him the Gunsmith."

Her hands flew to her mouth.

"Isn't he a gunman? A killer?"

"Some say . . ."

"Oh, my . . ."

"Worried?"

"About Abby," Rebecca said.

"Why?"

"It's obvious from the way she looks at him that she likes him very much."

"I see."

"I think he might hurt her."

"You mean . . . really hurt her?"

"I don't mean physically," she said, "but she's been here a long time, without a man."

"I see. Will she listen to you?"

"I don't know," Rebecca said, "but I'll have to try. He *is* very attractive."

"To you?"

She smiled and touched his shoulder.

"No, not to me." She leaned over and kissed him. It annoyed him because he was eating, but he didn't let it show.

"I better go back down."

"Will you say something to her now?"

"No, not now," she said. "Later."

"I tell you what."

"What?"

"Why don't you ask Adams to come up here and meet me after breakfast?" he asked. "Then you can talk to your friend downstairs."

"That's a good idea," she said. "You'd do that for her?"

"No," Cord Hardin said, "but I'll do it for you."

TWENTY

When Clint finished his breakfast Rebecca said, "Cord would like to meet you."

"Really? That's flattering."

"Is it?"

"Well, sure," Clint said. "After all, he's a famous man."

"He is?"

Clint stood up.

"Can I go up now?"

"Sure," she said. "It's the door at the end of the hall."

Clint said to Abby, "I'll be right back."

"I'll have another cup of coffee."

Clint went up the steps. They heard his footsteps as he went down the hall, and then they stopped.

Rebecca sat down.

"Do you know what you're doing?" she asked Abby.

"I was going to ask you the same thing."

"Why?"

"Do you know who Cord Hardin is?"

Rebecca sat back.

"Well . . . no."

"He's a bank robber, Rebecca," Abby said. "A bank robber and a killer."

Rebecca gave Abby an incredulous look.

"Do you know who Clint Adams is?"

"Yes," Abby aid, "I do."

"He's a gunman and a killer."

Abby sat back. She did not want to get into an argument with Rebecca while she tried to defend Cord Hardin.

"Look, Rebecca," Abby said, "both men have a reputation, but I don't have one of them in my bed."

"Yet."

"What's that mean?"

"I can see the way you look at him, Abby."

"I was up all night with his horse, Rebecca," Abby said.

"What were you doing all night?"

"Something I haven't done for years," Rebecca shot back, "and it was wonderful."

Abby hesitated before trying again.

"Rebecca, I'm sure it was wonderful to be with a man again," she said, "but . . . I don't want to see you get hurt."

"I'm a big girl, Abby," Rebecca said, standing up and picking up Clint's empty plate. "I think you're the one who had better be careful."

"Bec—"

"I have work to do."

Rebecca walked out of the dining room and into the kitchen. Abby debated following her, but decided to let it be for a while. Maybe she had given her friend something to think about.

And maybe she had some things to think about, herself.

Clint stopped in the open doorway and looked at Cord Hardin. The man wasn't in the bed; he was sitting in a chair by the window.

"I'm discovering that bed rest is not necessarily the best thing for cracked ribs," Hardin said.

"You might need to lie on something harder."

"Like the ground?"

"Maybe."

"You tellin' me to pull out?"

"Not my job," Clint said. "I'm not the law here."

"I understand your horse is down."

"He's doing better."

"Thanks to Abby, right?"

"Yes."

"You know why she's a vet now and not a doctor?"

"No, I don't. I don't know her that well."

"Maybe she'll tell you."

"Maybe."

"This is some coincidence," Hardin said, "me and my men here in this nothin' town the same time as you."

"I guess it is."

"I got no beef with you, Adams."

"I don't have one with you, either, Hardin," Clint said, "as long as you and your men don't do any damage here."

"Damage?" Hardin laughed. "Sounds to me that while I'm up here tryin' to heal my men are damaging each other."

"Seems that way."

"You know, Johnny Tolan—he's the one who did the shooting—fancies himself a quick hand with a gun."

"I got that impression."

"If he finds out you're in town—"

"And he will, right?"

"Hey," Hardin said, spreading his hands, "it's a very small town."

"I know."

"If I was you," Hardin said, "I'd watch my back."

"Why the warning?"

"I'm just tryin' to avoid trouble, Adams."

"That's what I'm doing, too.'

"You and me, we know how to avoid trouble," Hardin

said. "The Johnny Tolans of the world don't."

"Have your other men watch him."

"I tried that," Hardin said. "Quinn Butler's been with me a long time, and Johnny put a bullet in him. Ed Powell, he's been with me almost as long, and he don't want no part of Johnny. The other two . . . well, they're down, ain't they?"

"Looks that way."

"So nobody's ridin' herd on Johnny," Hardin said. "I'm just warning you, is all."

"I appreciate it."

"And if you find you have to kill him . . . well, don't worry about me and my men. That'd be Johnny's business, if he wants to go after you."

Clint frowned for a moment, then said, "I think I get it."

"Do you?"

"You want me to kill him."

"Why would I want you to kill one of my men?"

"Maybe so he won't kill any of yours."

"That's silly, Adams," Hardin said. "I'm just givin' you a friendly warnin'."

"Okay," Clint said, "so now I'll give you one."

"Go ahead."

"Leave this town in peace, Hardin," Clint said. "Pull out as soon as you and your men are healed and leave these people be."

"You mean leave this town in one piece, don't you?" Hardin said, laughing.

"I mean what I said."

"They got a lawman here," Hardin said. "You just told me this ain't your job."

"I owe Abby Fuller."

"And she asked you to warn me off?"

Clint didn't answer.

"You know my history with Abby?"

"I don't need to know anybody's history," Clint said. "I deal in today."

"Ask her, just for fun," Hardin said. "I mean, when you and her finish with your fun."

"This conversation is over."

"You mean you ain't had her yet?"

"Get well, Hardin," Clint said, turning to walk away. "Get well soon."

"Hey, Adams," Hardin shouted as Clint went back down the hall, "maybe when I do get well and on my feet I'll buy you a drink, huh? What about that?"

Clint kept walking.

TWENTY-ONE

When Clint came back down he and Abby simply left the house without speaking. They spoke only when they were walking back toward the center of the little town.

"What happened?" she asked.

"We danced."

"What?"

"Around each other," he explained, "like two bulls. What about you?"

"I warned her about him, she warned me about you."

"About me. But we're not sleeping together."

"Yet."

"What?"

"That's what Rebecca said," Abby added, hastily, "yet."

"Oh."

"What else did Cord say?"

"He warned me about Johnny Tolan."

"Who?"

"The kid who did the shooting."

"Why?"

"He says that when Tolan finds out I'm here he's going to want to try me."

"How will he find out?"

"Hardin will tell him."

"But why?"

"He wants me to kill the boy."

"Why?"

"I guess he's not fitting in with the rest of the gang," Clint said. "He seems a little . . . hotheaded."

"Something Cord Hardin has never been," Abby said.

"What will you do about your friend?"

"I don't know," Abby said. "I guess I'll leave her alone for a while, let her think."

"Has she been without a man long enough to . . . overlook a few things?"

"Probably."

"Did you tell her he was a killer?"

"Yes," Abby said, "but she told me you were one."

Clint didn't respond.

"I don't necessarily believe everyone's reputation, Clint."

"That's good."

"But I have more than reputation to go on when it comes to Cord Hardin," she said. "I know the man."

"You knew him."

"I spent five minutes with him," she said, "and I can tell he hasn't changed."

"Are you going back to the livery?" he asked.

"Yes," she said, "I want to check on Duke before I go and get some rest."

"Mind if I come along?"

"Be my guest."

While she was checking Duke over she asked, "What did he say about me?"

"What makes you think he said anything about you?"

She gave him a look.

"Are we going to dance now?"

"No," he said, "sorry. He just told me to ask you about your history with him."

"And are you?"

"No."

"Why not?"

"We don't know each other well enough yet for me to pry into your business," he said.

"I appreciate that."

"Don't mention it."

She backed away from Duke and looked him over.

"He's lost weight lately, hasn't he?"

"Some," Clint said. "I guess I should have noticed something sooner, but he's always been so . . . so . . ."

"Indestructable?"

"Exactly."

"Well, not anymore, Clint," she said. "He's worn out. He's just too old to go traipsing to hell and gone with you, anymore."

"I know," Clint said.

"What will you do?"

"I know someplace I can take him where they'll care for him," he said.

"Then what? Will you settle down, too?"

"Not me," he said. "I'll just have to find a new horse."

"That'll be pretty hard," she said, "after this one. I can tell how great he was just by looking at him."

"Great," Clint said. "He had it all, speed, stamina . . ."

"He deserves a rest now."

"Yes."

"And so do I."

"I agree there, too."

"I'm going to sleep for a few hours," she said. "What are you going to do?"

"I'll be around."

"I'll see you later, then."

"All right."
She started out the door, then stopped and turned.
"Do me a favor?"
"Sure."
"Don't get shot while I'm asleep?"
"Believe me," he said, "I'll do my best."

TWENTY-TWO

Johnny Tolan woke to a loud knocking on his door. He tumbled out of bed, tripped as the bedclothes got wrapped around his feet and almost fell headlong into the door before finally opening it.

"What the hell—"

"Time to see Cord, Johnny," Ed Powell said.

Tolan glared at Powell from behind bloodshot eyes.

"You're lucky I'm not wearin' my gun, Ed."

"Gonna shoot me, Johnny?" Powell asked. "That'll leave you as the only member of the gang not wounded. You'd have to take care of all of us, then. You up to that?"

"I'm no nursemaid," Tolan groused.

"Then get dressed," Powell said. "You can see Cord and have breakfast at the same time. That Mrs. Bradford is a damn good cook."

Tolan didn't know that, because he had never gotten around to eating last night.

"Well," he said, clutching his stomach, "I am kinda hungry."

"I'll wait for you outside," Powell said. "You and me's the only ones who can walk over to the rooming house to eat. We'll have to bring some food back for the others."

"Huh? Oh, yeah, sure."

"And when we do that," Powell said, "you can make your apology to Quinn for shootin' him."

"Oh, yeah," Tolan said, "that. Okay, okay, I'll meet you out front in half an hour."

"Make it ten minutes," Powell said. "I'm starvin'."

"Okay, ten minutes," Tolan said. "Geez." And he slammed the door.

Powell walked down to Butler's room and let himself in.

"Did you wake him?" Butler asked from his bed.

"Yeah."

"Is he in a foul mood?"

"Kinda," Powell said. "I thought his mood would be worse after all the drinkin' last night."

"His mood only has to be bad enough to get him shot," Butler said, "either by Cord, or by the Gunsmith."

"Well, that rooming house is the only place to get breakfast," Powell said. "Maybe Adams'll be there."

"Probably not," Butler said. "It's kinda late, you know. He's probably been up for hours, checking on his horse."

"Well" Powell said, "there wasn't any reason for us to get up early, was there?"

"Nope," Butler said. "No reason at all."

"I'll wait outside for Johnny and take him over to Cord."

"Just make sure he don't shoot you, too," Butler said.

"I'll be careful."

When Johnny Tolan appeared out in front of the hotel he was smiling. Powell hadn't expected that. He and Butler had talked it over the night before, before either of them went to sleep. They thought Tolan would be in a bad enough mood to get himself shot. And here he was, smiling.

"What're you so happy about?" Powell asked. "You're about to get your ass reamed by Cord for shootin' Quinn."

"I don't know," Tolan said. "I just got this feelin' that today's gonna be my day."

"Well then, let's get over to the rooming house and get it started," Powell said. "A good breakfast and a good ass-reaming and you'll be on your way to a great day."

"You can't ruin my mood, Ed," Tolan said. "I just feel so damn good, I can't explain it."

Powell shook his head and said, "Let's go."

When Rebecca appeared in the doorway to her bedroom Hardin had gotten himself back into her bed.

"Are you all right?" she asked.

"I'm fine. Are they gone?"

"Yes."

"Good," he said. "My men should be comin' over for breakfast and I don't want them runnin' into the Gunsmith."

"Is he really the Gunsmith?"

"Yes, he is. Why?"

"I'm worried about Abby being involved with him," Rebecca said. "I don't want her getting hurt."

"She a good friend of yours?"

"Yes," Rebecca said, "ever since she came here about ten years ago. We've always had a lot in common."

Hardin was thinking that she and Abby had even more in common now, only Rebecca didn't know it.

"You will fix breakfast for my boys, won't you?" he asked.

"Of course," she said. "I'll go downstairs right now and get started, Cord."

"You're a good woman, Rebecca."

Of course, he never did know how to treat a good woman.

TWENTY-THREE

Rebecca was very uncomfortable with the way Johnny Tolan looked at her. The young man made no secret of what he was thinking. It was plainly written on his face—and if it hadn't been, his words filled in the blanks.

"So there aren't many women in town, huh?" he asked Rebecca on one of her trips from the kitchen.

"I'm afraid not."

"So what do the men do, you know, for fun?"

"I'm sure I don't know," she said, and retreated into the kitchen.

"Lay off her, Johnny," Powell said.

"Why should I?"

"Because she and Cord have gotten close."

"Cord's getting some of that?" Tolan asked. "Lucky man. Maybe I'll try my luck with that lady vet, huh?"

"If you're finished with your breakfast," Powell said, "you better go upstairs and try your luck with Cord."

"You know, Ed," Tolan said, throwing his napkin down on the table, "you're almost no fun at all these days."

"It's the room at the end of the hall," Powell said, as Tolan went up the stairs.

Tolan made his way down the hall to the room and peered in. Hardin was lying in bed, looking real old to Tolan.

"Don't even think about it, Johnny."

"About what, Cord?"

"About takin' me while I'm lyin' on this bed," Hardin said.

"Why would I be thinkin' that?"

"Why would you shoot Quinn Butler?"

"He pushed me, Cord," Tolan said. "You know I don't like bein' pushed."

"I'm gonna push you, Johnny," Hardin said, "right out of this gang if you don't shape up. You can't go shootin' other members of the gang. It's bad for business—and for morale."

"Okay, okay," Tolan said, "I won't shoot nobody else."

"Okay, Johnny."

"From the gang, that is."

"What's that mean?"

"Did you hear who was in town?"

"Who?"

"Clint Adams, the Gunsmith himself."

"Stay away from him, Johnny."

"Why?"

"Because he'll kill you."

"Him? He's as old as y—well, he's kinda old."

"Old don't mean slow, Johnny."

"Cord," Tolan said. "I'm fast, you know I am. I could take the Gunsmith, easy."

"Johnny, I'm warnin' you," Hardin said, knowing that warning Johnny Tolan away from something was like pushing him toward it, "stay away from Adams. He's too good for you."

Tolan bristled.

"You shouldn't be sayin' things like that, Johnny."

Hardin watched Tolan carefully for some sign that he was going to draw.

"I'm just telling you for your own good, Johnny," Hardin said. "That's all. It's just advice. You can take it or leave it."

"I think I'll leave it."

"That's up to you."

"You got anything else you want to say to me, Cord?"

"No, Johnny," Hardin said. "That was all."

"I'll get goin', then," Tolan said. "I got the feelin' I got a big day ahead of me."

As Tolan turned and walked down the hall Hardin took his gun out from beneath the bedclothes. It would probably be good for everyone concerned if Johnny Tolan did go after the Gunsmith and get himself killed. Couldn't have somebody in the gang you couldn't trust, and just the fact that Hardin had felt he needed to be holding his gun while talking to the younger man made it clear enough that he didn't trust him.

Go ahead, Johnny, he thought, *go after the Gunsmith.*

When Tolan came back downstairs he left the house right away without a word. Powell went up to see Hardin.

"Is he gone?" Hardin asked.

"Left here with a real determined look on his face."

"How are the boys?"

"They're all doin' real good, Cord. Your gal friend is a real good doctor, for a vet."

"She's not my gal friend," Hardin said, quickly. "Just somebody I used to know."

"Okay, sorry," Powell said, backing off, "but she did do a real fine job of patchin' the boys up. Will and Ben should be ready to ride in a day or two, but Quinn might need more time, since his wound is new. How about you? How're the ribs?"

"Comin' along," Hardin said. "I'll be ready soon, and Quinn will be ready when I am."

"Where we headin' after this?"

"I ain't decided, yet. See what you can do, though, about gettin' enough supplies for a few days when we leave."

"Right," Powell said, "I'll check in at the general store. I don't expect they'd have much to pick from in a town this size, but we can probably get what we need for a few days until you decide where we're goin' when we leave here."

"Good," Hardin said, "and stay out of Johnny's way. He's a hair trigger, right now."

"I better get goin'," Powell said. "The others'll be gettin' hungry. I'll check back with you later."

"If somethin' happens," Hardin said, "check back with my right away, you hear?"

"I hear ya, Cord."

Powell headed for the door of Hardin's room, and Rebecca—who had been listening at the top of the stairs—hurried back down before she could be seen. She'd heard enough to know, however, that Cord and Abby knew each other from someplace before Firecreek. She just wasn't sure what she was going to do with that piece of information.

TWENTY-FOUR

After Clint had spent a few hours with Duke in the livery he started to think it was safe to leave the big gelding alone. His breathing was a lot better than it had been. Abby Fuller seemed to have worked a miracle overnight, and he had made a promise to her—a promise he meant to keep, which he couldn't do cooped up in the stable all day.

"Petey, you going to be around here all day?" Clint asked.

"That's my job, Mr. Adams," Petey said. "Why? You want me to do somethin' for ya?"

"Yes, I do."

"What?"

"I want you to stay around here all day and keep an eye on Duke."

"Oh," Petey said, disappointed, "well, I reckon I can do that, all right."

"I'll be around town," Clint said, "so I won't be hard to find if something goes wrong with him. Just be sure you run for Doc Fuller before me. Okay?"

"Yes, sir."

"Oh, and Petey, where's Doc Fuller's office?"

"Doc don't got no office, but she's got a room over the general store. You got to go into the alley to get to it."

"Okay, thanks."

"Anythin' you want me to do, Mr. Adams, you just let me know and I'll do 'er."

"How about calling me Clint?"

"Yes, *sir*. I can do that for sure."

"Good," Clint said. "Then I'll see you later, Petey."

"Okay . . . Clint!"

He was shaking his head as he left the livery. The boy sure was eager to please.

Clint decided to go and talk to the part-time sheriff again, Ben Pepper. Truth be told, there just wasn't much else to do, and maybe he could price some supplies for himself. He also wanted to find out if he could buy a horse anywhere nearby. He didn't want to ride Duke a foot if he didn't have to.

When he entered the general store there was a man there ahead of him who also seemed to be pricing supplies. It only took a moment for him to realize the man was going to be buying for four or five. That, and the worried look on Pepper's face as he entered, told him this was one of Cord Hardin's men. Then, when he got a look at the man's face, he realized this was the man who had helped Abby get the wounded man back to the hotel after he'd been shot in the livery.

"How's your friend doing?" Clint asked.

The man turned and looked at him.

"Are you talkin' to me?"

"Your friend," Clint said, "the one who got shot yesterday? How's he doing?"

"That's right," the other man said, "you were there."

"I came by just after it was all over."

"He's doin' okay," the man said. "That pretty lady doc fixed him right up."

"That's good."

Now the man turned and faced him and Clint noticed he wasn't wearing a gun.

"You're Clint Adams, ain't you?"

"That's right. What's your name?"

"Ed Powell. I heard a lot about you."

"Half of it's probably not true."

"Well, if *only* half is true..." Powell said, but didn't finish. His meaning was clear.

"Well," Clint said, "don't let me interrupt. I'm just going to look around a bit."

"That's okay," Powell said. "I was just pricin' some supplies for when we leave."

"And when do you think that would be?" Clint asked.

"Oh, probably not until Cord Hardin is ready to ride."

"And the others?"

"They'll ride when Cord's ready."

"Really?" Clint asked. "They've all been shot, and he's got bruised, maybe cracked ribs, and they'll be ready when he is?"

"Or get left behind," Powell said.

"I see. Uh, don't you have one more man who isn't wounded?"

"Tolan," Powell said, "Johnny Tolan."

"Ah, yeah, he's the one who shot your friend."

"Johnny's a hot head," Powell said. "He's gonna apologize to Quinn today. Quinn Butler, that's my friend's name."

Neither the names Powell nor Butler meant anything to Clint.

"It would take a lot more than an apology to make it better if somebody shot me," Clint said.

"Well, Quinn's pretty understanding, and I guess Johnny could've killed him."

"That's one way to look at it, I guess," Clint said. "A pretty generous way."

"I guess," Powell said. He looked at Ben Pepper and said, "I'll let you know when I need those supplies, friend."

"They'll be ready." Powell turned to Clint. "Nice talkin' to ya."

"You, too."

Ben Pepper and Clint both watched the man walk out of the store, then looked at each other.

"Don't seem to be lookin' for trouble, does he?" Pepper asked, obviously relieved at the outcome of the two men's confrontation.

"No, he doesn't," Clint said. "It would be nice if it stayed that way, too."

"You got reason to believe it won't?"

"Not right now, I don't," Clint said. "Not right now."

TWENTY-FIVE

Ed Powell found Johnny Tolan sitting on a wooden chair in front of the hotel.

"What are you doin'?" he asked.

"Just sittin'."

"The way you lit out of the rooming house I thought you were lookin' for somebody."

Tolan stared up at Powell and smiled.

"You and Cord must think I'm stupid."

"Why do you say that?"

"Quinn, too," Tolan said. "I'll bet he's in on this."

"In on what, Johnny?"

Tolan laughed.

"You all think you can get me to go off half-cocked, go after the Gunsmith and get myself killed."

Powell was taken aback. He didn't think Johnny Tolan was smart enough to figure that out.

"Why would we want you to do that, Johnny?"

"To get rid of me."

"Because you shot Quinn?"

"Not because of that," Tolan said.

"Then why?"

"Because you're all afraid of me."

"Why are we afraid of you?"

"Well, Cord because he thinks I'm gonna take over."

"And me and Quinn?"

"Because you think I'll take over and you'll have to take orders from me," Tolan said.

"And because of this we want you dead?" Powell asked. "Why wouldn't we just kill you ourselves?"

"Well," Tolan said, scratching his nose, "you and Quinn can't, you're not fast enough."

"And Cord?"

"He might, eventually," Tolan said, "if Adams doesn't do the job for him first."

"And what happens to our big plan if you kill Adams?" Powell asked.

"Well, I don't know for sure, Ed," Tolan said, standing up, "but I sure hope to find out." He stepped down from the boardwalk into the street, then turned and said, "That's what I aim to make happen—but in my own time."

Powell watched Tolan walk away and wondered how they had all managed to underestimate him.

TWENTY-SIX

"You're pretty well stocked here," Clint said.

"And that surprises you?" Ben Pepper asked.

"Frankly, yes."

"Well, I go into Star Forks every month and stock up, because after you leave Star Forks we're the only other place to get supplies for miles, going North."

"I see. And when you leave town who takes over as part-time sheriff?" Clint asked.

"Nobody," Pepper said. "You see, I'm part-time sheriff because this town hardly ever needs the services of a lawman. That's the only reason I took the damn job."

"I understand the town owns the livery?"

"That's right," Pepper said, glad to change the subject.

"I'm going to need a horse when I leave here."

"There are a few you could look at," Pepper said, "but none that would be what you're used to."

"All I need right now is transportation."

"Do you want to look at them now?"

"No," Clint said, "not now, not until I've got in mind a definite day to leave, and until I know where I'm going. If it turns out I don't like what you've got, is there anyplace else to buy?"

"Only one place," Pepper said. "The Cullen place, about ten miles north of town."

"On the way to Star Forks?"

"That's right."

"Could I rent an animal from you, ride it there, buy one and then leave yours there to be picked up later?"

"How would we get it back?"

"You could pick it up during one of your trips to Star Forks for supplies."

"I suppose I could," Pepper said.

"Well," Clint decided, "let's discuss that after I've seen what you have."

Clint turned and walked to the window of the store. Across the street he could see Ed Powell talking to the younger man, Johnny Tolan. He wondered if Powell was telling Tolan where he was, aiming him over this way. After a few moments he saw Tolan get up and walk away, and guessed not.

"Do you want any supplies now?" Pepper asked.

"No," Clint said, "I'm like the Hardin gang. I can wait." He turned and looked at Pepper. "Seems to be enough supplies here for everyone. I'll come and see you when I want to look at those horses ... Sheriff."

Pepper made a face and said, "I'd appreciate it if you wouldn't call me that."

Clint left the general store without replying.

Johnny Tolan was proud of himself. At least now Powell knew—and he'd tell both Butler and Hardin—that he wasn't as dumb as they thought he was. It was after he left Hardin's room, and the rooming house, and came over to the hotel to sit that he figured it out. It made perfect sense to him. The whole gang—well, not so much Taylor and Packer, but for sure the other three—were all afraid that he was going to take over the gang. They saw Clint Adams being in town as a chance to get rid of him. That's because they were not only underestimating how smart he was, but also how fast he was.

Oh, he was going to face the Gunsmith before either of them left town, but it was going to be in his time and on his terms. He liked the idea of Hardin, Butler and Powell waiting around to see what he was going to do.

It put him in control, which was a place Johnny Tolan liked to be.

TWENTY-SEVEN

"Well, he surprises me," Quinn Butler said, when Ed Powell told him about his conversation with Johnny Tolan. "I didn't think he was that smart. I thought he was all mouth and short fuse."

"Well, he ain't."

"This could still work, though."

"How?"

"He's still gonna go after Adams," Butler said. "I know it. He can't resist."

"So we just wait?"

"Maybe," Butler said, "we can stack the deck a little."

"How do we do that?"

"You go and talk to Adams."

"You mean warn him?"

"That's what I mean."

Powell was quiet.

"You got a problem with that?"

Powell was still quiet.

"If you do, talk to Cord," Butler said. "He'll make it an order."

"I don't mind standin' around and watchin' them shoot

it out to see which one falls," Powell said, "but the kid's been ridin' with us for a while, Quinn."

"So?"

"So I kinda feel like I'd be puttin' a bullet into him myself."

"It sure didn't bother him to put a bullet into me," Butler pointed out. "You think it'll be any different with you, or Ben, or Will next time he gets mad?"

"Probably not," Powell said.

"I tell you what," Butler said, swinging his legs to the floor, "you and me will go and see Adams together."

"Are you up to it?"

"I wouldn't miss it," Butler said. "Get me my pants, will you?"

Clint went back to the livery after talking with Ben Pepper and found Petey stroking Duke's neck. This showed him how truly *unlike* himself Duke really was. He hardly ever let anyone touch him that way.

"How's he doing?" Clint asked.

"He's gonna be fine," Petey said. "He sure is big."

Clint eyed Duke critically and realized the gelding had lost a lot of weight.

"I wonder if he'll eat?" he said aloud.

"I tried to feed him," Petey said, "but he wouldn't take any. Maybe later."

"Maybe," Clint said. Before he could even think about taking Duke anywhere the big horse was going to have to put back some of the weight he'd lost. He'd have to talk to Abby about that.

He was about to say something to Petey when he heard somebody entering the stable from behind him. He turned and saw Ed Powell and Quinn Butler. Both were armed. Butler had told Powell he wasn't going on the street without his gun, so Powell had put his back on.

"Relax, Adams," Powell said, realizing Clint was looking at their sidearms. "Nobody's here for trouble."

"Then why are you here?" Clint asked.

"To avoid trouble," Butler said, "or, better yet, to warn you."

"About what?"

"Johnny Tolan."

"I know all about him."

"Not *all* about him," Butler said. "He's out looking for you right now, Adams."

"I doubt that."

"Oh? Why?"

"Because this is not a big town," Clint said, which was an understatement. "If he was really trying to find me it wouldn't be hard. So I think your warning is a little premature."

"I wouldn't take Johnny lightly if I was you," Butler said.

"Oh, I'm not taking him lightly," Clint said. "In fact, I'm not taking him at all—at least, not until the time comes."

"You'd do better to find him before he finds you—"

"Why are you fellas in such an all fired hurry for him and me to square off?" Clint asked. "Could it be that you want me to do your dirty work for you?"

Butler and Powell exchanged a glance, and then Butler asked, "Whataya mean?"

"I think you know what I mean," Clint said. "Go back and tell Hardin that if he really wants Tolan dead he should do it himself. I'm going to do everything I can not to have a confrontation with him."

"I don't think you'll be able to do that, Adams," Butler said. "He *is* determined to kill you. He's just going to pick his own time."

"Can't say I blame him for that," Clint said. "At least when he comes for me I'll know his intentions. It's when

I don't know people's intentions that they make me nervous."

Butler and Powell exchanged another glance.

"I think you boys better back on out of here," Clint said. "I'm starting to get nervous."

TWENTY-EIGHT

"Wow," Petey said from the hayloft, after Hardin's two men left the livery. "You really made them back off."

"They backed off because they weren't ready to do anything, Petey," Clint said. "How long have you been up there?"

"A little while."

"Come on down."

"Yessir."

Instead of using a ladder to come down Petey simply dropped down from the loft, landing athletically on his feet.

"I'm going to see about getting another horse," Clint said. "Will you see if you can get Duke to eat anything while I'm gone?"

"I'll try."

"Maybe I'll also wake up Doc Fuller and see what she has to say about it."

"Okay."

"I'll be back in a while."

"I'll take care of him."

Clint was surprised to see the big gelding nudge the boy's arm until Petey started rubbing his neck.

Definitely not the same old Duke.

113

• • •

Cord Hardin thought that Rebecca Bradford's skills in bed were improving by the minute. Maybe it was just that she had gone without for so long, but she really seemed to be getting more and more confident, and eager. She was crouched between his legs now, cupping his testicles lovingly in one hand, while licking his shaft up and down and stroking his thighs with the other.

She was sucking him wetly, making noises that were getting him more excited. Finally, he felt as if his penis had swelled so much it was going to burst. He reached down and pushed her off of him. She fell back onto her heels, panting, her eyes shining, staring at him.

"What's wrong?"

"Too fast," he gasped, "I don't want it to end yet."

She smiled and said, "Me, neither," reaching for him.

Her breasts were heavy, with large, brown nipples. The skin was smooth and pale. They had some sag to them, he noticed, but that was all right. She wasn't exactly a young girl—not that he wanted a young girl at his age.

Ten years ago, when he had been involved with Abby Fuller, she had not been a young girl either, but they were both younger, and they both thought they had something. It was only after she found out what he did, what he *was* that she left. He understood that, then. It's not every woman who can warm to the fact that her man robs people for a living and sometimes, in the course of a robbery, has to kill. That was his business, though, what he was good at, and he wasn't about to give it up for a woman.

He hoped that Rebecca Bradford knew that. He hoped she wasn't starting to think that he might stay in Firecreek after he was healed. There was absolutely no chance of *that*. He also hoped she wasn't thinking about going with him when he and the boys left. That wasn't going to happen, either.

What was going to happen, though, over the next few days, was that he was going to enjoy her, ribs or no ribs.

He reached for her and she came to him, pressing her breasts to his face so he could lick them, bite them. He slid his hands over her body, touching her, probing her, causing her to grunt and moan, grow wet and pungent...

This was all he wanted her for—well, this, the bed, a place to heal, and some food—and when he was done he'd be on his way.

Later Rebecca sat on the edge of the bed, getting dressed.

"What's wrong?" he asked, because she was quiet. One thing the woman could do was talk, so when she was quiet, he noticed.

"Nothing."

"Ain't it just like a woman to say nothing's wrong when something is?" he commented.

"Have you known a lot of women?"

"A few, over the years."

She hesitated, then said, "Like Abby Fuller?"

"So that's it," he said. "How did you know?"

"I heard you talking to one of your men." She looked at him. "Is that why you came here? Because Abby's here?"

"Yes."

"Do you love her?"

He made a sound with his mouth and said, "No. We came here because we needed patching up and I knew she could do it."

"But she's a vet."

"She wasn't always a vet."

"What?"

"When I knew her she was a doctor," he said, "but Abilene wasn't ready for a lady doctor."

"So she became a vet?"

"I don't know," he said. "I lost track of her after Abilene, only heard of a lady vet here in Firecreek a few months ago."

"And you knew it was her?"

"No, but she always wanted to help animals as much as people," he said, "so I checked it out."

"Why? If you aren't in love with her?"

"Because," he said, "doing what we do, the boys and I sometimes need mending. I try to keep track of where we can go for it without running into law."

"We have a sheriff."

He made the noise again and said, "A part-time sheriff. I'm not worried about him."

"So you're not still . . . I mean, you aren't going to try to get her back?"

"Get her back?" he said, laughing. "I never had her, Rebecca. Abby doesn't want me, and I don't want her. If I did, would I be here with you, now?" He put his hand on her shoulder.

"No," she said, pressing her cheek to his hand, "I suppose not."

"So," he said, removing his hand, "how about something to eat, then?"

TWENTY-NINE

"Things are not working out," Butler said to Powell, after they left the livery.

"I guess we better tell Cord," Powell said.

"No, not yet," Butler said. "There's got to be a way to fix this so that Adams kills Johnny."

Powell looked at Butler.

"You really want this to happen, don't you?" he asked. "You're not taking this bullet in the shoulder as lightly as you wanted me to think, are you?"

"Would you?" Butler asked. "That young pup coulda killed me, Ed. I ain't gonna stand still for that."

"So what do you want to do?"

"Are you with me?"

"Well," Powell said, "if it comes down to a choice between you or Johnny, yeah, I'm with you."

Powell didn't add that if it came down to Butler or Hardin, that would be a different matter, but he didn't think he had to. Butler would probably feel the same way.

"So what do we do?"

"Maybe," Butler said, "we can give Adams a reason to go after Johnny . . ."

• • •

Clint was trying to decide whether to go into the general store, or up to Abby Fuller's door to wake her up when the decision was made for him. Abby came around the corner from the alley, stopped when she saw him, then smiled and continued on.

"Have you had enough sleep?" he asked.

"Enough to function," she said. She smelled good, like she had washed her hair and bathed with some scented soap. "How's Duke doing?"

"To tell you the truth, I'm worried," he said. "He's not eating anything."

"He might not eat until tomorrow," she said, 'but I'll take a look at him. If you were worried, why didn't you wake me?"

"You needed the rest," he said, "although I was this far from waking you when you came around the corner. You have good timing."

"That's never been the case before now," she said. "What are you doing about another horse?"

"I was going to talk to Pepper about that."

"Don't bother," she said. "Talk to Ansel Willis. He has a place just outside of town."

"The same place Pepper told me about?"

"Probably. Ans has probably got an animal you can use for a little while, until you find something better."

"How do I get there? Walk?"

"It's a little far to walk," she said. "If you can wait until I've looked at Duke I can hitch up my buggy and take you out there. I'd give you my horse, but she's really not fit to ride."

"No, no," he said, "that's okay. I can wait. In fact, I'll walk back with you."

"Fine."

They fell into step together. Clint liked how tall she was

when she was wearing her boots. She had her hair down now instead of up, and it hung past her shoulders.

"What?" she asked, as if sensing he was looking at her.

"Your hair smells good."

She touched it, but didn't say anything. He thought the comment might have alarmed her in some way, so they walked the rest of the way in silence.

THIRTY

After checking Duke and deciding he was fine with Petey watching, Clint and Abby hitched her horse to her buggy and drove him out to Ansel Willis's place. Willis was a short, very bowlegged man who had spent most of his life around horses, and had the scars—and some missing fingers—to prove it.

"Sure," he said, after Abby had introduced them, "I got some stock you can look at. Come out back."

Willis's house was a shack that he had built himself which was maintained by his wife, who peered at them through the window but did not come outside.

"She's shy," he said.

He walked them around back to an equally hand-built corral with about eight or nine horses in it, all of them fine-looking stock.

"You breed these yourself?" Clint asked.

"Gotta do something to make a living. These are all three and four years old. I got five colts, and four fillies. Take your pick and we'll dicker on a price. I'll give you time to take a look."

"Thanks, Mr. Willis," Clint said. "I appreciate this."

"The Mrs. and I will be expectin' both of you to take supper with us," the man said.

Clint looked at Abby, who nodded.

"All right," Clint said. "We'd like that."

As Willis walked away Abby said, "You saved yourself some money by agreeing to stay for supper. That was part of the dickering."

"Thanks for the clue."

Clint opened the corral, entered and closed it behind them. The horses parted as he walked among them, examining them critically. He stopped by two of them to run his hands up and down their legs, then came walking back to where Abby was waiting.

"Which one do you like?" he asked.

"I like that dappled grey filly over there."

"She's a nice one," he said, "but too young."

"He said they were all three or four."

"Well, she's not," he said. "Maybe this is part of the dickering, also, to see if I could pick her out."

"Which one do you like, then?"

"There are two colts over there who might fit the bill," Clint said. "One of them is small, but would have a lot of speed, the other is bigger, and would have staying power."

"Which do you prefer?"

"Well," he said, "I've always been spoiled by Duke having both of those qualities," he said, "but if I had to pick one, I guess I'd go with the staying power."

"Well then," she said, "pretend you like the small one better, and you'll probably get a better price on the big one."

"Well," he said, "you sure sound like you know how to dicker."

"I've done it a time or two," she said.

Clint came out of the corral and Willis was nowhere in sight yet, so he leaned on the gate and looked at Abby.

"What are you hiding from, Abby?" he asked.

"That's a real personal question," she said.

"You're helping me pick out a horse," he said. "That's pretty personal, too."

"It's not the same thing."

"I know."

"I could ask you what you're running from."

"What makes you think I'm running from anything?"

"You're usually on the move, aren't you?" she asked. "Never stay in one place for too long?"

"That's pretty much right," he said, "but I don't see it as running *from* something."

"I do."

"From what, then?"

"Commitment?"

"You mean, to a woman?"

"A woman, a place," she said, "it doesn't matter. You don't like to commit yourself to anything for too long. It seems obvious to me."

"I see."

"Am I right?"

He thought a moment.

"I guess you are, in a way," he said. "I certainly can't seem to stay in one place for very long. I just get an urge to move, you know? To be on the trail."

"And you don't think that's running from something?"

He thought another moment and then shook his head. "No, I can't say I agree with you. I just enjoy being on the move, on the trail, seeing new places, new faces, revisiting some old ones . . . no, I think you're wrong, Abby. I'm not running from anything."

"Well," she said, "if I'm wrong, I'm wrong."

"So?"

"So what?"

"Am I wrong?"

"About what?"

He smiled. "About you hiding from something."

"Here comes Ansel," she said, "prepare to dicker—and no, you're not wrong."

THIRTY-ONE

"What if we just kill him?" Powell asked.

"What?"

Butler and Powell were watching Ansel Willis's place, waiting for Clint and Abby to head back to town.

"Why would we do that?"

"Why fool around?" Powell asked. "We could kill him and we'd get the reputation."

"Are you nuts?" Butler asked. "I don't want every gunny in the country comin' after me because I killed the Gunsmith."

Powell scratched his jaw and said, "Yeah, I guess you're right."

"We just want him to think that Johnny took a shot at him, that's all," Butler said. "You've got to take the shot because I can't fire a rifle with this shoulder."

"Okay," Powell said, "okay, it's just that I'm not used to shooting to miss."

"Do the best you can," Butler said, "and even if you manage to hit him, don't kill him!"

Clint and Ansel Willis dickered and came to an agreement.

"What happened to your horse?" Willis asked, but before

Clint could reply he added, "I jest figured, the doc bein' here with you, somethin' must have happened to him."

"He's being retired," Abby said, "for his own good."

"I've heard about him for years," Willis said. "Must have been a good animal."

"Still is," Clint said, "he's just come to the end of the trail, I guess."

"We all do," Willis said, "sooner or later. Well, come inside and we'll do the paperwork for the sale, and then we'll have dinner. The wife's shy, but she's a helluva cook."

They followed Willis into the house.

"How long they gonna be here?" Powell asked, impatiently. "It's gonna be dark, soon."

"So what?" Butler asked. "You need light to shoot at him and miss?"

"I guess not," Powell said, grudgingly.

"Then just settle down," Butler said.

Willis was right about his wife's cooking. The only thing Clint found better than the food was the coffee afterward.

Over dinner Willis agreed to keep the horse in his corral until Clint was ready to leave town.

"Any idea when that'll be?" the older man asked.

"You'd have to ask the doctor that, Ansel," Clint said. "She knows Duke's condition better than I do."

"It probably won't be for a few more days," she said. "We have to get him eating again."

"Well, if anybody can fix him up it's Doc Fuller," Willis said. "Best damn horse doctor I ever saw."

Clint found it odd but that comment seemed to bother Abby rather than flatter her.

Willis walked them out to Abby's carriage and waved as they drove off.

"What's wrong?" Clint asked.

"What do you mean?"

"When he called you the best damn horse doctor he ever saw I thought you'd at least look flattered," Clint said. "Instead, you looked . . . sad."

She looked at him, then back at the trail. He gave her a few moments to compose her thoughts.

"Well?"

She sighed.

"I guess I just don't think that 'horse doctor' is a real compliment," she replied.

"You mean because you treat all animals?"

"I mean," she said, "because I'm not really a vet. My training was as a doctor."

"You mean . . ."

"As a physician," she added. "Yes."

Clint was about to ask her to explain when there was a shot. The horse reared and the carriage threatened to tip. Clint threw his body across Abby's to protect her, while at the same time trying to control the horse. However, the second shot thoroughly spooked the animal. He reared again, broke free and this time the carriage did tip. Clint and Abby were thrown to the ground, and now he was trying *not* to land on her.

They hit the ground together and he heard the air rush from her lungs. He rolled, drew his gun and came to a stop in a crouch, the gun held out in front of him, and waited for a third shot so he could locate the muzzle flash.

It did not come.

ST. MARYS PUBLIC LIBRARY
BOX 700   15 CHURCH ST. N.   ST. MARYS
ONTARIO   N4X 1B4

THIRTY-TWO

When a third shot was not forthcoming Clint turned to look at Abby, who was lying flat on her stomach.

"Are you all right?"

She lifted her head and looked at him.

"Yes, you?"

"I'm not hit."

"I'm bruised," she said, "but not shot."

They both remained silent for a moment, listening.

"Are they gone?"

"It seems so," he said. "They, he, whoever." He stood up and holstered his gun, then reached down to assist her in standing. She brushed herself off.

The buggy was lying on its side and the horse was gone. He was about to say something when he heard someone approaching from the way they had come. He drew his gun again, but it was Ansel Willis, on foot, carrying a rifle.

"I heard the shots," he said. "Are you both all right?"

"We're fine," Clint said. "A little bruised, but fine."

"It'll be dark soon," Willis said. "Come back to the house. You can stay the night."

"If we can borrow a horse," Clint said, "we can right the

buggy and hitch it up. I'd like to get back to town tonight."

"Well," Willis said, "I can rent you a horse."

Clint looked at the man and asked, "For how much?"

Willis shrugged and said, "We can dicker."

"You're a real businessman, Ansel."

"I try."

They made their deal to rent a horse and hitched it up after checking to make sure the buggy was in one piece. Once again they started for town with Abby driving.

"So what was that about?" she asked.

"I don't know."

"Does that happen to you a lot?"

"Yes."

"It's a hell of a way to live."

"Tell me about it."

"Do you have any ideas who it might have been?"

"I know who somebody wants me to think it is."

"Who?"

"Johnny Tolan."

"The young man who shot one of his own gang?"

"Yes."

"Why don't you think it was him?"

"Because I know his type."

"Which is?"

"When he comes for me it will be head on," Clint said, "face to face, not from ambush."

"And what makes you so sure of that?"

"He fancies himself a hand with a gun," Clint said. "Those kind of men have to prove it all the time."

"I saw him draw," she said. "He is fast."

"All the more reason to believe it wasn't him."

"Then if it wasn't him, who was it?"

Clint looked at him and said, "Someone else."

• • •

When Powell and Butler got back to town they took their horses back to the livery. Petey was up in the loft. He had watched them and listened while they had saddled their horses earlier, and now he did the same while they unsaddled their horses.

"Do you think they're hurt?" Powell asked.

"Who knows?"

"A fall like that could have broke their necks."

"I doubt it," Butler said. "We'll find out soon enough."

They finished with their horses, but before leaving stopped in front of the stall inhabited by Duke.

"That's his horse," Powell said.

"I know."

"What are you thinkin'?"

Butler rubbed his jaw. Petey decided that if they tried to hurt Duke he'd have to stop them.

"Nothin'," Butler said. "Come on, let's get out of here before they get back."

"Maybe they won't be back tonight?" Powell suggested.

"They'll be back," Butler said. "Adams is gonna want to know who took those shots at him, and he's gonna want to know tonight. He'll be back."

"So what do we do in the meantime?"

"We find Johnny," Butler said.

THIRTY-THREE

It was dark by the time Clint and Abby got back to town. The streets were hardly lit and if not for the moon probably would have been pitch black. As they approached the livery, though, they saw two lights. One was from the livery itself.

"Where is that other light from?" Clint asked, as he helped Abby down from the buggy.

"The saloon—or what we have that passes for a saloon."

"Ah."

"Are you thinking you'll find somebody there?"

"Somebody."

"But who?"

"That's the question. Can you unhitch the horse yourself?"

"Don't you want to check on Duke?"

For a moment he was torn between that and trying to find out right away who had taken the shots at them—at him!

"All right," he said, finally relenting, and they went inside.

"I saw them!" Petey said, right away, agitated. "I heard them, and I saw them!"

"Calm down, Peter," Abby said. "You saw who?"

"The two men who rode after you, and came back before you," he said.

Abby looked at Clint, who took over the questioning.

"Who did you see, Petey?"

"I saw the man who got shot, and the other man—the one who helped you take his friend to the hotel, Doc."

"Powell and Butler," Clint said. "I'm not surprised."

"They took the shots at us?" Abby asked.

"They shot at you?"

"I'm sure of it," Clint said.

"They shot at you?" Petey asked, again.

"But why?" Abby asked.

"To make me think it was Johnny Tolan, so I'd go after him," Clint said.

"And then what?"

"And then either I would kill him, or he'd kill me."

"Why do they want you dead?"

"I don't think they do," Clint said. "I think they figure on me killing the kid."

"They shot at you?" Petey asked again.

"Petey!" Abby shouted, annoyed with the boy. He backed off like a kicked puppy.

"I'm sorry, Petey," she said, reaching out to touch his shoulder. "Yes, they shot at us, but we're fine."

"Petey, what did they say when they were saddling up?"

"They were talkin' so fast I couldn't tell," Petey said, "but when they came back they was wonderin' if somebody had broke their necks and died. Was that you?"

"Yes, Petey," Clint said, "that was us. Our buggy tipped over, but we're fine."

"What're ya gonna do?" Petey asked. "You gonna shoot them?"

"No," Clint said, "I'm going to talk to them, Petey."

"And what about the other one?" Abby asked. "Johnny Tolan?"

"I'm wondering if maybe they took a shot at him, trying to make him think it was me," he said. "Petey, was there any shooting here while we were gone?"

"Nope," Petey said, shaking his head, "no shots at all."

"Okay," Clint said, "so they didn't do that. Petey, you help Abby with the horse—by the way, did her horse come back here?"

"No," Petey said, "I ain't seen it."

"Must be wandering around in the dark" Clint said. "Petey, help Abby unhitch her buggy."

"Where are you going?' Abby asked.

"Over to that saloon," Clint said. "I want to see who I'm going to find there."

She grabbed his arm and said, "Be careful."

"I always am."

Powell and Butler saw Johnny Tolan sitting at the one table in the little saloon and trading post.

"Should we go in?" Powell asked.

"We ain't got time," Butler said. "Adams is gonna be back soon. Let him find Johnny here."

"And then what?"

"And then maybe they'll shoot it out," Butler said. "Come on, my shoulder is startin' to hurt. I got to get some rest."

They started walking away from the saloon toward the livery, but stopped short when they saw somebody coming their way.

"Duck," Butler said, and they each found a dark corner to hide in while Clint Adams walked by, apparently on his way to the saloon.

"Still want to go to bed?" Powell asked.

"No," Butler said, coming out of his hole, "let's stick around here and see what happens."

THIRTY-FOUR

Clint opened the door and entered the unmarked saloon/trading post. Instead of a bar there was a door set on two barrels, forming a counter. Behind it a man leaned with his jaw in his hand. There was one table in the place and there was one man sitting at it.

Johnny Tolan.

Clint approached the "bar" and the man perked up enough to open one eye.

"You got beer?" he asked.

"Sure."

"I'll have one."

The man drew it and set it on the bar. It looked flat, and when he tasted it, it was warm.

"Thanks."

He took the beer and walked to the small table, which had one empty chair right across from Tolan.

"Mind if I sit?"

Tolan, who had been watching him since he came in, asked, "And if I say no will you sit somewhere else?"

"Doesn't seem to be somewhere else," Clint said.

"Sit."

Clint sat.

"Beer tastes like piss," Johnny Tolan said, "but it's all this town has got."

Clint sipped it, then put it down and pushed it away.

"You ain't gonna drink it?"

"Not a chance."

"You mind if I do?"

"It's yours."

The younger man moved it over to his side of the table.

"Soon as I finish this one."

"You must be desperate for beer."

"Just for somethin' to do," Tolan said. "What brings you over here, Mr. Adams?"

"Somebody took a shot at me tonight."

"That right? Did they miss?"

"Twice."

"Couldn't've been me, then," Tolan said. "I wouldn't have missed."

"I don't think you would have shot at me from cover, anyway," Clint said.

"You got that right."

"You'd come right at me."

"Right again," Tolan said. "So if you know it wasn't me, who do you think it was?"

"Somebody who wants me to think it was you."

"And why would they want that?"

"I think you can answer that as well as I could, Johnny," Clint said. "You mind if I call you Johnny?"

"I don't mind," Tolan said. "we should be on a first name basis, seein' as how I'm gonna kill you."

"Makes sense, I guess."

"So tell me who you think shot at you?"

"You partners, Powell and Butler."

"Why?"

"They want us going up against each other," Clint said, "probably because you shot Butler."

"That's only part of it," Tolan said, "but you're right, they do want us goin' up against each other—and it's gonna happen."

"It doesn't have to."

"Yeah, it does."

"I was afraid you were going to say that."

"Why?" Tolan asked. "You ain't afraid of me, are you?"

"Hardly."

"That's good, 'cause I ain't afraid of you, either."

"Listen," Clint said, "why should you give those boys exactly what they want?"

"I ain't," Tolan said.

"How do you mean?"

"Well, they want you to kill me," Tolan said.

"So?"

"That ain't what's gonna happen," Tolan said. "See, they're afraid of me, so they want me dead, but after I kill you, they'll be even more afraid of me. That *ain't* givin' them exactly what they want, is it?"

"Not if it comes out the way you want it to."

"It will."

"How can you be so sure?"

"I'm good."

"So am I."

"You *were* good," Tolan said. "I *am* good. There's a difference."

"You think you're better than me because you're younger?" Clint asked.

"Yup," Tolan said, "although, I also think I'm better than you ever was."

"That's an awful lot of confidence you're carrying around with you," Clint said.

"I can handle it."

"Well," Clint said, "I just wanted to make sure you didn't come at me half-cocked. As long as we both know we're not going to shoot each other in the back we can do this at our leisure, and not when somebody else wants us to."

"If you was gonna drink your beer," Tolan said, "I'd drink to that."

"That's okay," Clint said, getting up, "you can drink to it for both of us."

Clint Adams left the saloon, walked off toward the livery, then turned down the street, probably walking to the hotel. Powell and Butler came out of their holes again.

"Nothin' happened," Powell said.

"Yeah, it did."

"What?"

"They talked."

"That's all?"

"That's enough," Butler said. "We better talk to Cord tomorrow."

"Why?"

"Because if we don't," Butler said, "we're dead."

"How do you figure?"

"If they talked they probably both figured out what we were doin'," Butler said.

"Shit."

"That's right," Butler said. "We better stay away from both of them until we talk to Cord. He'll know what to do."

"Christ," Powell said, "I hope so."

THIRTY-FIVE

Clint went to his hotel, figuring Abby would have already left the livery. On the way to the hotel it struck him that going back to his room was like stepping into the midst of a nest of vipers. Just down the hall were the rooms of two men who had taken shots at him. Granted, it was doubtful that they were trying to kill him, but still . . .

He was passing the general store and noticed it was closed. As he passed the alley he saw the stairway up the side of the building that led to Abby's rooms, and saw a light in the window. He decided to go up and see if she was still awake. After all, she'd only had a nap that afternoon after staying up all night with Duke. She was probably still tired.

He knocked on her door and waited. She opened it and smiled when she saw it was him.

"You're all right," she said.

"I'm fine."

"I found some bruises," she said, "but I'm fine, too."

She had changed her clothes and was now wearing a simple cotton dress. The way it molded itself to her body, and the way her breasts moved, he could tell she was wearing nothing underneath.

She fidgeted a bit beneath his stare and said, "I didn't plan on going out again, so I just . . . put this on."

"I was going back to my room," he said, "but the hotel . . ."

"Oh," she said, putting her hands to her mouth, "it has only four rooms, and in the other rooms must all be Cord Hardin's men."

"Right."

"Including the ones who shot at us."

"Right again."

"Well," she said, "you could go to the rooming—but Cord is staying there."

He nodded.

"Well . . . would you like to come in for coffee and tell me what happened at the saloon?"

"I thought you'd never ask."

She backed away and allowed him to enter, then closed the door.

"This is nice," he said. He was standing in a living room, sparsely but comfortably furnished.

"I have three rooms," she said. "There's also a bedroom and a kitchen."

"A nicer place than I've seen in some big towns."

"I know," she said, "I was surprised when I got it. Come into the kitchen. I've already made coffee."

He followed her into the kitchen, which had a small table with two chairs.

"I don't entertain much," she said. "Two chairs is plenty. Please, sit down."

She poured two cups of coffee and brought them back to the table.

"You're probably very tired and I'm keeping you up," he said.

"No," she said, "not at all. I'm curious to hear what happened at the saloon."

So he told her about his conversation with Johnny Tolan, and she listened in rapt attention until he was done.

"He actually said he was going to kill you?"

"Yes."

"And that doesn't worry you?"

"No."

"Why not?"

"Because I've heard it from young men, many times before."

"And?"

"And what?"

"What happened?"

"They didn't kill me."

She hesitated, then asked, "Because you killed them?"

"When I couldn't talk them out of it."

"And how often did you try to do that?"

"Every time."

"And . . . how often did you succeed?"

"Not very often," Clint said. "What are you trying to get me to say here, Abby? That I've killed men before? Fine, I've killed men before. Young men, old men, and it was usually when they were trying to kill me."

"Like Tolan?"

"Yes, like Johnny Tolan," Clint said. "I'll try to talk him out of it, too. I'll give him every opportunity to withdraw. If he doesn't, though, I'll kill him rather than let him kill me. Would you expect me to do anything less?"

"No," she said, "I suppose not."

He sat back in his chair and regarded her for a moment.

"I'm not Cord Hardin, Abby," he said, "if that's what you're afraid of. From what I know of him he's killed men, usually during the commission of a bank robbery. That's very, very different from what I've done."

"I understand."

"Do you? I hope so," Clint said. "I'd hate to think I have to prove myself to you."

"You don't," she said.

"Good," he said. He stood up. "Maybe I should leave."

"No," she said. "What you say is correct. You're not Cord Hardin, I know that."

"Tell me the answer to my question," he said.

"What question?"

"The one I asked out at Willis's, before we went in to have dinner. Have you forgotten?"

"No."

"I'll repeat it, anyway," he said. "What are you hiding from, Abby?"

THIRTY-SIX

"I knew Cord Hardin in Abilene years ago," she said. "I was fresh out of medical school, and determined to be accepted in the West as a physician."

"In Abilene?"

"I know," she said. "I found out it was an impossible task. But at the same time I was quite taken with Cord, because I didn't know what kind of man he was. When I found out, I felt like a fool—twice over."

"Twice?"

"For believing everything he told me," she said, "and for thinking I could force people to accept me."

"So what happened?"

"I left Abilene, very disillusioned."

"And became a vet?"

"No," she said, "in fact I never became a vet. My training is still as a physician. I simply tried some other places, other towns, moving around in the hopes of finding one that would let me practice—and trying to find a place where Cord Hardin wouldn't find me."

"And you eventually ended up here?"

"Eventually," she said. "I arrived here and there was a

man with a sick horse here. I knew what was wrong with the animal, and I cured it. In fact, it was similar to the problem your Duke was suffering. The people asked me to stay."

"There were more people then?"

"Oh, yes," she said. "That was four years ago, and there were a few more, but this never was much of a town. People would stop here, though, on their way to or from Star Forks. They'd make use of the general store, and they'd make use of my talents as a 'vet.' "

"So you never told anyone you weren't a vet," he said. "You simply set up practice."

"And was accepted," she said, "finally."

"And are you happy with that acceptance?" He knew the answer to that. If she were she would not have flinched when Ansel Willis called her a "horse doctor," the day before.

"No," she said. "I was for a while, but it's starting to wear off."

"What do you want to do?"

"I haven't decided."

"And how has seeing Cord Hardin again affected you?"

"Hardly at all," she said. "I don't have any feelings for him or about him anymore. I . . . I'm worried about what will happen to you, being stuck here with him and his men."

"Well," Clint said, "they had a clear shot at me tonight, and missed on purpose."

"What do you think they'll do?"

"Well, my best guess would be they'll go to Hardin in the morning and tell him they messed up."

"And what will he do?"

"Yell at them, berate them, and tell them to just wait and see what happens between me and Tolan. My feeling about Cord Hardin is that he's not an impatient man."

"He wasn't when I knew him," she said. "I would think he'd only become more patient with age."

"That's what I think."

"But you don't want to go to the hotel, do you?"

"I figure why put temptation in their path," he said. "No, I think I'll spend the night in the livery, with Petey and Duke."

"No," she said, "you don't think that."

"What?"

"Why did you come up here?"

"I saw your light on, wanted to make sure you were all right."

"No."

"Why do you keep saying no?"

"That's not why you came up here."

"Okay, if you're so smart," he said, "why did I come up here?"

She stood up, walked to him, put her arms around his neck, tugged his head down—she was shorter, now, without her boots—and kissed him.

"That's why you came," she said, moments later.

"No," he said, sliding his hands beneath her dress, "not just for that..."

THIRTY-SEVEN

They moved into the bedroom together and he slid his hands up her thighs, bunching her skirt, then brought it all the way up over her head. With her hands up in the air like that her breasts lifted and presented themselves to him. He palmed them, rubbing the nipples with the center of his palms, then closed his hands over them, then slid his hands beneath them to cup them and heft their weight. She was full bodied—a woman's body, with a waist, wide hips, a full butt, a body built for days and nights in bed with a man. He didn't have days and nights to spend with her, but he had hours, and he intended to put them to good use.

She undressed him, then, kissing each inch of bare flesh as she exposed it, until he was naked and she was on her knees in front of him. She cradled his swollen cock, rubbed it against her cheeks and lips, then used her tongue to wet him before sliding him into her mouth. Some men thought that this was the whore in every woman, but Clint just thought that this was the *woman* in every woman.

She suckled him until he was ready to burst, then he lifted her to her feet by slipping his hands beneath her arms. He took her to the bed and laid her down, then began to explore her body with his hands and mouth. Her skin smelled of a combination of her last bath and the day's perspiration, a heady combination to him. He reveled in it, gave her as much pleasure as he could with his hands and tongue before mounting her, sliding into her and then moving in and out of her with long, slow strokes. She gasped, slid her legs up around his waist, kissed his face and neck and shoulders and then, as her body shuddered, sank her teeth into him to keep from screaming . . .

Cord Hardin decided that his ribs were never cracked or broken, only bruised—otherwise, how could he do what he was doing now. He was crouched between Rebecca Bradford's legs, his penis buried in the steamy depths of her. He had an ankle in each hand and was spreading her as wide as he possibly could, and was driving himself into her powerfully, causing her gasp and moan and possibly even cry out in pain—but he didn't care. He was caught up in his own feelings, his own pleasure, and he continued to slam into her even as the back of his mind was telling him it was time to move on tomorrow. Since this was to be his last night with her, he was going to treat her like a whore he'd never see again after this . . .

"Stay the night," she said, later, as they lay side-by-side. "I'd hate for you to go back to the hotel and get killed."

"That sounds like an offer I can't refuse."

"Why don't you leave tomorrow, Clint?" she asked. "Take the horse you bought from Willis and leave Duke with me. I'll take care of him. After Cord and his gang leave you can come back, or send somebody back, for him."

"It's something to think about, Abby," he said, although he had no intentions of doing it. When he left Firecreek Duke was going to leave with him.

She rolled over and put her head on his shoulders, pressed the length of her body against his. He slid an arm around her and nestled his chin against the top of her head. A man could get used to this, if he let himself. Sleeping with a woman every night was not the worst thing that could happen to a man—although a lot of men would say not the *same* woman. Still, to do that you'd have to live in the same town day in and day out, and it was that he wasn't ready for, more than anything else.

"What are you thinking?" she asked.

"Just about possibilities."

"Your heart is beating very fast."

"That's because of you, doctor," he said, "and what your hand is doing beneath the sheets, at the moment."

"Oh?" she asked. She pressed her lips to his ear. "Is my hand doing something?"

THIRTY-EIGHT

"I'm glad you boys came over this morning," Hardin said to Powell and Butler.

"Why's that, Cord?"

"Because I came to a decision last night," Hardin said. He had made up his mind just before his final blow had knocked Rebecca Bradford unconscious.

"What decision?"

"That having Clint Adams here in town is more than a coincidence," Hardin said. "It's an opportunity that's too good to pass up."

"Whataya mean, Cord?" Powell asked.

"I mean," Hardin said, "that if he's dead when we leave here, the rep for killing him can carry us a long way. Banks would open their vaults for us willingly."

"But . . . what about him killin' Johnny?" Butler asked.

"We'll kill Johnny," Hardin said, "after he helps us kill Adams. The credit for killing the Gunsmith will go to the whole Hardin gang."

"What about your ribs?" Butler asked.

"They're fine," he said. "A little sore, but they must have been bruised, not broken. And lying in that bed has given me a taste for some action."

They were sitting around the table in the dining room and now Rebecca came out carrying a tray of breakfast for the three of them. Bradford and Powell could see by the bruises on her face that Hardin had given in to the urge for action sometime during the night, as well.

Rebecca served them, then went into the kitchen and started crying. She'd thought that Hardin was going to kill her last night, and now she wasn't so sure he wouldn't before he and his men left. How could she have been so fooled by him? Beneath all the charm had been a killer all along.

"Eat your breakfast," Hardin said, "and then we'll go and get the boys. Was Adams in his room when you left the hotel?"

"Don't know," Butler said. "We didn't check."

"That's okay," Hardin said. "In a town this small he can't hide for very long."

Somehow, Quinn Butler wasn't sure that the Gunsmith would be trying to hide at all.

Johnny Tolan woke to the sound of men walking in the hall. He opened his door a crack and saw Butler and Powell walking away. No doubt they were going to see Cord Hardin.

Tolan decided that today would have to be a big day in his life. He was going to have to make some hard decisions for himself, ones that would set him on a path he would follow for the rest of his life.

He closed his door, turned and started to dress.

When Butler and Powell returned to the hotel it was with Cord Hardin, who looked rested, and was wearing his gun. Tolan was sitting in front of the hotel in a wooden chair.

"Cord," he said, "it's good to see you up and about. How are the ribs?"

"They're fine, Johnny," Hardin said, "thanks. Quinn, you and Ed go in and get Will and Ben—and check with the clerk and see if Adams is still in his room."

"Right, Cord."

There was another chair nearby so as Butler and Powell went into the hotel Hardin pulled this chair over and sat next to Tolan.

"Johnny, what are your plans for the Gunsmith?"

"I'm gonna kill 'im, Cord," Tolan said. "I know you and the boys think he's gonna kill me—hell, he even thinks that—but believe me, it's me that's gonna do the killing."

"Let me propose something to you," Hardin said.

"What?"

"That we all kill him," Hardin said. "All five of us."

Tolan looked at Hardin.

"That wouldn't be a fair fight."

"Fair fight be damned, Johnny," Hardin said. "We'd be the gang that killed the Gunsmith. That's all I care about. Banks would be so intimidated by that they'd be begging us to take their money."

Tolan wasn't hearing anything about money.

"I want to kill him in a fair fight," Tolan said. "What's the use of killin' him if I don't get his reputation?"

"Johnny," Hardin said, "let me see if I can make you see this my way—"

"No, Cord," Tolan said, "forget it. I'm killin' him."

Hardin studied the younger man stolid profile for a few moments before speaking again.

"Okay," he said, slowly, "but it'll have to be today. We're pullin' out."

"Are the boys ready to ride?"

"I'm ready," Hardin said. "Anybody who ain't can stay behind."

"We hardly been here two days at all," Tolan said. "I thought you needed to get some rest."

"I rested enough," Hardin said. "I felt like an old lady lying in that bed. I need to get me some action, and I doubt that Clint Adams bein' here is an accident. It's a Godsend."

"Yeah," Tolan said, "for me. Let me ask you somethin', Cord."

"Go ahead."

"Do you think you can take me in a fair fight?"

"Sure."

"And Adams?"

There was the slightest hesitation before Cord said, "Yes."

Tolan stared at Hardin, incredulously.

"You're more confident that you can take me than you are that you can take him?"

"I can take both of you, Johnny," Hardin said. "I hope you ain't gonna make me prove that."

Tolan took his eyes off of Hardin and sat back in his chair.

"I don't know, Cord," he said. "I just don't know what I'm gonna do."

Abby looked out the window of her bedroom and then called to Clint.

"You better come and see this."

He came to the window, buttoning his pants, still bare chested as he was in the middle of getting dressed.

"Hardin and that young one," she said, pointing across the street.

"Johnny Tolan," Clint said. "What's Hardin doing up and about? I thought he had broken ribs."

"They could have just been bruises," she said.

While they watched the other four members of the gang came out of the hotel and Hardin started talking to them.

"This looks bad," Abby said.

"Maybe they're going to leave."

"You really believe that?"

"No," Clint said. "I was wondering when Hardin was going to start thinking the way Johnny Tolan is."

"You mean . . . about killing you?"

Clint nodded.

"It'd be a feather in his cap—in the cap of the whole gang—if they could be the ones to kill me."

"How can you be expected to face six men?" she demanded.

"I don't think I'll have to."

"Why not?"

"Because Johnny Tolan wants me for himself," Clint said. "I don't think he'd be party to six against one."

"Oh, Lord," she said, suddenly.

"What's wrong?" he asked.

"Rebecca," she said. "What did he do to Rebecca?"

"What makes you think he did anything to her?"

"There's something I didn't tell you about my past with Cord," she said. "The last time I saw him, he almost beat me to death."

THIRTY-NINE

"He ain't in there," Butler said, when he came out with Powell, Packer and Taylor.

"What?" Hardin asked.

"That ain't all," Powell said. "He didn't come in at all last night."

"Think he's hidin' out?" Taylor asked.

"No," Hardin said, "not him. He don't hide."

"Then where is he?" Butler asked.

Hardin thought a moment, then said, "He's with her."

"Who?" Powell asked.

"Abby Fuller."

"The vet?" Butler asked.

"That's right," Hardin said. "Find her and you find him." He looked at Butler. "Where does she live?"

"I don't know—"

"Well, find out."

"How?"

"How?" Hardin bellowed. "Ask, that's how. Ask that part-time lawman who runs the general store, ask that idiot who works at the livery . . . why do I have to tell you everything? Ask!"

"Okay, Cord," Butler said, "okay. Me and Taylor will go ask the livery kid, Powell and Packer can ask the sometime sheriff. That do you?"

"Just do it," Hardin said. "Johnny and I will wait here."

"Why does Johnny get to stay here?" Taylor demanded.

"Because I don't want him out of my sight," Hardin said. "Now get movin'!"

Clint and Abby left her rooms, went down the stairs and then around behind the buildings so they could make their way to the rooming house without being seen. Clint did not want anyone else opening fire on him with Abby in harm's way.

"Why didn't you tell me this before?" he demanded. When she'd first told him how Hardin had beat her he had almost gone right out into the street.

"Because I saw the way you've been looking at me," she said. "You would have gone after him."

"You think so, huh?"

"I know so."

"How was I lookin' at you?"

"The way a thirsty man looks at a water hole," she said.

"Wow," he said, "we think a lot of each other, don't we?"

"I think last night bears me out, Clint."

"Oh," he said, "right . . ."

The banter was to keep Abby's mind off of her friend, Rebecca. When they reached the rooming house the front door was unlocked. They went in and found Rebecca on the floor in the living room. Her face was bruised, there was blood coming from her mouth, and she was unconscious.

"Jesus," Abby said, bending over her and examining her. "He beat her during the night, and then hit her again before he left."

"Is she going to be all right?"

"I don't know," she said, "I can't tell. Carry her to her room and put her on the bed."

He did as he was told while Abby went to the kitchen. He put Rebecca on her bed and Abby came walking into the room carrying a basin of water with some rags beneath her arm.

"I've got to stay with her," she said.

"That's good," he said. "It'll keep you out of the way."

"What are you going to do?" she asked, without looking at him. She was sitting on the bed, cleaning her friend's face.

"Get this over with, I guess," he said. "The tension in the air is starting to get to him."

She looked over her shoulder at him and said, "Somehow I doubt that."

"Well," he said, "it's time to get it done, anyway."

"You're going out there? Six against one?"

"Maybe I can get the sheriff to help."

"I doubt that."

"Besides, I told you," he added, "it won't be six. Johnny Tolan won't help them."

"He looked pretty chummy sitting there with them."

"Abby," he said, "just stay inside and do what you do best. I have to go outside and do what I do best."

"What, kill?"

He answered, "No, stay alive."

FORTY

Once again staying behind the buildings, Clint made his way back to the general store over which Abby lived. She told him there was a back door that was never locked, and he found it with ease. He entered and found himself in a storage room. There was a curtained doorway in the opposite wall, and when he went through that he was in the store.

It was a mess. Merchandise had either fallen or been pulled down from the shelves, and lying in the middle of the store, partially covered, was Ben Pepper, the town's part-time lawman.

Clint rushed to the man and bent over him. He'd been beaten, but was still alive.

"Pepper," Clint said, pulling the man into a seated position, "Pepper, what happened here?"

"Two men..." Pepper said, haltingly "... wanted to know where Abby lived... if you were with her..."

"Did you tell them she lived upstairs?" Clint asked, shaking the man. "Did you?"

"I couldn't help it," he said. "They woulda killed me."

"Did you hear what happened?"

"They went upstairs," he said. "I could hear them break in, and then break up the place. Was she there? Is she all right?"

"She's fine," Clint said. "What else did they say?"

"They said that two other men were asking Petey the same questions at the livery."

"Petey . . ." Clint said.

He went to the front door but saw Hardin and Johnny Tolan still sitting across the street. Making his way back through the storeroom, no longer concerned about the welfare of Ben Pepper, he ran out the back and started running toward the livery, hoping he'd be in time . . .

When he got to the livery he went in the front way, heedless of the fact that two of Hardin's men might still be there. In fact, wanted them to be there. His anger was reaching the boiling point.

However, there was only one man there and it was Petey, lying in the middle of the livery, his face a mass of blood. Clint bent over him and knew immediately that he was hurt much worse than Ben Pepper. He knew why, too. Pepper had talked, and Petey would die before he'd give up Abby Fuller's location.

In fact, he still might.

FORTY-ONE

Clint returned to the rooming house carrying Petey, who he knew was hurt badly. He shouted for Abby as he entered and she came running down from upstairs.

"What happened to him?" she demanded.

"He was beaten," Clint said, "probably because he wouldn't tell Hardin's men where to find you."

"Oh, my God," she said. "Bring him upstairs to one of the rooms."

"How's Rebecca?" he asked, as he followed her up.

"She's going to be all right," Abby said. "She just feels humiliated."

Clint followed Abby down the hall to one of the rooms and deposited Petey on one of the beds.

"Jesus," she said, "stay with him while I get something to clean him up with."

Clint stared down at the bloodied, unconscious young man and knew that he had not kept his promise to Abby to keep the town safe from Hardin and his men—but he was going to.

When Abby came back in and started cleaning Petey up he said, "Ben Pepper was beaten, too.'

"Bad?"

"No," Clint said, "he didn't hold out the way Petey did."

"He's a foolish boy," Abby said of Petey.

"He was trying to protect you."

"By getting himself killed?" she asked. "That's just stupidity."

"Or courage."

"What are you going to do now?" she asked.

"I think," Clint said, "that after they've looked all over town for us—and that won't take long—they won't have any choice but to come back here."

"What do we do then?"

"I guess we'll have to fight them," Clint said. "Does Rebecca have a gun, or a rifle, in the house?"

"Her husband's rifle should be here, somewhere," Abby said. "Probably downstairs."

"All right," Clint said. "I'll find it and then keep watch out the front window. You keep working on the boy. Can you tell how badly he's hurt yet?"

"Not yet."

"Well," Clint said, "you'll fix him. After all, you're a hell of a doctor."

"Helluva horse doctor," she reminded him.

"No," he said, "I just mean a hell of a doctor."

She turned to look at him over her shoulder, but he was gone.

FORTY-TWO

Clint found Rebecca's husband's rifle, an old Henry, and a box of shells. It would do. He carried it to the front of the house and looked out the window. There was nobody in sight, so he settled down to wait.

If they came in the back, he was in trouble.

"He's got to be at the rooming house," Hardin said.

"Why there?" Powell asked.

"Because we've looked everywhere else...haven't we?" Hardin asked, giving everyone the same hard look.

"Yeah, we have," Powell said.

"And the two women are friends," Hardin went on, "Abby and Rebecca, so that's where they'd go."

Hardin stood up, looked down at Johnny Tolan.

"We're goin' over there, Johnny," he said. "Are you comin'?"

Tolan hesitated a moment, noticed everyone was looking at him, sighed and stood up.

"Yeah, I'm comin'."

Abby came downstairs and joined Clint in the front of the house.

"How are they?"

"Resting," she said. "They'll both be all right. Petey will take longer to heal than Rebecca, but they should both be all right."

"Thanks to you, Doctor."

"Give me the rifle," she said. "I'll cover the back."

"Abby—"

"Somebody's got to cover the back, Clint," she said. "If they come that way we'll be in a lot of trouble, right?"

"Right," he said. "Do you know how to shoot?"

"Yes."

"Have you ever shot anyone?"

"No," she said, "I've never even shot *at* anyone."

"Well," he said, handing her the rifle, "there's a first time for everything."

She took the rifle.

"Don't fire unless they're trying to actually enter the house," he told her.

"All right."

"And call out the minute you see anything."

"Right."

He pulled her to him and kissed her.

"Good luck," she said.

"To both of us."

When the five men came within sight of the house Hardin held his hand out for them to stop.

"Ed, take Will and Ben and go around back. See if you can find a way inside."

"Right."

"Quinn, you, Johnny and me will take the front. I'm gonna try to talk Adams out first."

"Why?" Butler asked. "Why don't we just go in?"

"Because we won't all make it to the door alive," Hardin said. "Do you want to be the one to die?"

"No."

"I didn't think so." Hardin looked at Powell and the other men. "Well, go!"

"We're goin'," Powell said.

As the three men worked their way around to the back of the house Hardin said to Butler and Tolan, "We'll give them a few minutes to get into place."

He turned to look at them both, but saw only Butler.

"Where the hell did Johnny go?"

FORTY-THREE

Abby ran to the kitchen door, called out to Clint in a loud whisper, "There are three men in the back."

"Get back to the window!" he snapped. "I've got two up here." Where, he wondered, was Johnny Tolan?

"Adams!" Hardin called. "Clint Adams!"

"I hear you, Hardin."

"Send the women out, Adams," Hardin said. "There's no need for them to get hurt."

"You hurt one of them enough that she can't walk, Hardin," Clint said. "You like beating up women, I hear."

Silence.

"Then you come out, Adams, and face me."

"I'd face you in a minute, Hardin," Clint called back, "but you've got a little too much help out there to suit me."

"They won't interfere," Hardin said. "It'll just be you and me."

"You can't possibly think I'm that dumb, Hardin."

"Whataya mean?"

"You haven't got the guts to stand against me alone."

Apparently, that made Hardin mad because he began firing at the house, followed by the man—Butler—who was with him. As if on signal the three men behind the house also started firing.

"Stay down!" he shouted to Abby, hoping that she could hear him over the sound of glass and dishes shattering.

After a few moments the barrage stopped, probably because they had to reload.

But then there were a few more shots, and no accompanying glass breaking. They sounded like they came from the back.

"Clint!" Abby shouted.

"What's happening?" he asked.

"They're down," she said. "The men back here are down."

"Shot?"

"I don't know," she said. "I thought I saw one of them get shot, but I can't tell."

What the hell was going on?

What the hell was going on? Hardin wondered.

"Who's shootin'?" he demanded of Butler.

"I don't know," he said. "Should I go and find out?"

"No," Hardin said, "stay here with me."

They finished reloading, and Hardin called out to Clint again.

"Adams!"

Clint didn't answer. He thought this would drive Hardin crazy. He skittered across the living room to the kitchen door.

"What's happening back there?"

"I-I don't see anyone," Abby said. She was peering out the window of the back door, which had lost most of its glass. Clint took the chance of crossing the room to also look out. She was right. There was nobody back there.

"Adams! You hear me?"

Suddenly, Johnny Tolan appeared in the back.

"What's he doing?" Abby asked.

"I don't know."

Tolan walked around behind the house and stopped three times to look down, move something with his feet. After the third time he looked at the door, as if he was looking right at Clint, shrugged and walked away.

"What?" Abby said.

"He killed them," Clint said, incredulously. "Damn. He killed the three of them."

"But . . . but why?"

"I told you he wouldn't be a party to this," Clint said. "He's evened the odds."

"Even?" she asked. "There are still two of them out there. And him."

"Come on," Clint said, grabbing her arm. He pulled her along with him until they were both looking out the front door.

"Adams!"

"Hardin!" Clint called.

"I hear you."

"I'm coming out."

"You can't—"

"Just stay here and keep your rifle ready," he said.

"I can't watch your back!" she said. "I-I don't even know if I can hit anything."

"That's all right," he said. "If something goes wrong, just start firing to make noise."

"Clint—"

"It'll be over soon, Abby," he said.

He holstered his gun, stood up, opened the front door and stepped outside.

FORTY-FOUR

Clint was prepared for them to fire on him as soon as he stepped outside, but it didn't happen. He stepped down off the wooden porch and stopped.

Hardin and Butler moved forward, Hardin telling the other man, "Don't worry, we got him outnumbered."

"But the others are in the back—"

"They'll come out when they hear us," Hardin said. "Don't mess this up, Quinn."

"Where's Johnny?" Butler asked.

"That's what I'd like to know."

"Where are the rest of your men, Hardin?" Clint called out. "I can't believe you intend to face me two to one."

"I told you, Adams," Hardin said, his eyes darting about looking for his other men, "it could be just you and me."

"Don't make me laugh, Cord."

They all turned toward the new voice and saw Johnny Tolan come out from the side of the house.

"You thought you had a six-to-one advantage when you came here," Tolan said. "Well, now you don't. You're down to just two."

"What?" Butler asked. "Johnny, w-what did you do?"

"I evened up the odds, Quinn," Tolan said. "It's just you and Cord against Adams."

Butler looked at Hardin, panic in his eyes.

"Where are the others, Johnny?" Hardin asked.

"Dead."

"You . . . killed them?" Butler asked.

"I did," Tolan said.

"But why?"

"I told Cord I wouldn't watch Adams shot down by all of you," Tolan said. "He deserves to die in a fair fight."

"F-fair?" Butler stammered.

"Two to one, Quinn," Tolan said, "you and Cord against Adams. That sounds fair in my book."

"B-but, are you standing with Adams?" Butler asked.

"No," Tolan said, "I'm going to wait and see what happens, and then I'm going to kill the winner."

"B-but what if that's us?" Butler asked.

"Don't worry, Quinn," Johnny Tolan said, folding his arms across his chest, "it won't be."

Cord Hardin didn't know what to do. How could he be sure Johnny Tolan would stay out of the fight? How could he trust Butler to back him?

"Quinn?" he said. "We can do this."

"I d-don't know, Cord."

"Quinn!" Hardin said, his tone getting colder. "Don't you back out on me."

"Cord, I-I can't—" Butler broke and ran.

"Quinn!" Hardin shouted.

"Oops," Tolan said, "looks like it's just you and Adams now, Cord."

"Johnny," Hardin said, "listen to me. We can take him together, you and me. We can do it."

"Sorry, Cord," Johnny Tolan said, "I don't want to play

on your side anymore. This is the way it has to play out now."

"Walk away, Hardin," Clint said. "Just walk away."

"You don't get off that easy, Adams," Tolan said. "Whether he walks away or not you still have to face me."

"If you walk away, Hardin," Clint said, "I only have to kill one man today."

"Why don't I just watch you and Johnny, Adams?" Hardin asked. "How about that?"

"No way, Cord," Tolan said. "You don't get to watch. You get to go first. Oh, and one more thing."

"What?" Hardin asked.

"If you walk away, I'll come after you when I'm done with Adams. See, boys, one way or another, I'm the only one who's gonna walk away from this."

FORTY-FIVE

"Of course," Johnny Tolan said, "we could all draw at the same time."

Clint could see that the young man was enjoying himself. He was so supremely confident that he could outdraw these two "old" guns that he would even propose something as ludicrous as this.

"Who shoots who?" Hardin asked.

Tolan smiled.

"That's the fun part."

"Johnny," Clint said, "killing a man shouldn't be fun."

"Oh, but it is, Adams," Tolan said, "it is. Maybe that's why you don't like doin' it, but I do."

"How many men have you killed, Johnny?" Clint asked.

"Plenty."

"You're fast," Clint said, "and you've outdrawn men before—like Quinn Butler—but you haven't killed anyone yet, have you?"

"Tell him, Cord," Tolan said. "Tell him about the teller in that bank in Rimrock."

"An unarmed teller?" Clint asked. "That was fun? What about this, Johnny. Facing two men who want to kill you.

What if Hardin and I agree to take care of you first, and then each other?"

For the first time a look of doubt crossed the young man's face.

"I think I'll go back to my original plan," he said. "You two go first, and I'll watch."

Clint looked at Hardin.

"What about that, Cord?" he asked. "Are we going to do this Johnny's way?"

Hardin thought for a moment, trying to figure out who his best chance would lie with.

He decided it was with Clint Adams.

"I don't think so," Hardin said. "I kind of like your way, Adams."

"So first we kill Johnny, and then we face each other?"

"Or not," Hardin said. "we could kill Johnny and walk away."

"Wait a minute, wait a minute," Johnny Tolan said. "What does that accomplish? Cord, I thought you wanted the Gunsmith's reputation."

"I wanted it for the gang, Johnny," Hardin said, "but it looks like you killed most of the gang, and Quinn has run off."

"What about for yourself?"

"I don't need it," Hardin said. "I'll just put together a new gang and start over—after you're dead."

"This ain't fair," Tolan said. This wasn't the way it was supposed to happen, he thought.

"Your call, Johnny," Clint said. "Do we all draw, or do we all walk away?"

Hardin and Clint both turned to face Tolan while the kid made up his mind.

"Fine," he finally said, "we'll all walk away."

Clint could see Cord Hardin breathe a sigh of relief.

"Okay with you, Cord?" Clint asked.

"That's fine with me, Adams," Hardin said. "All I want to do now is get out of this town."

"And I'm going back in the house," Clint said.

He backed up until he could step up onto the porch, then heard Abby open the door behind him. He was almost inside when Johnny Tolan drew and shot Cord Hardin square in the chest. With a surprised look on his face Hardin fell forward, dead.

Tolan holstered his gun and changed his position so he could see Clint.

"Don't bother going inside, Adams," he said. "It's just me and you, now."

"Johnny," Clint said, "haven't you killed enough men today?"

"Not nearly enough," he said. "I got room for one more."

"Clint," Abby said, from behind him, "just come inside."

"He won't leave it alone, Abby," Clint said. "I know his type."

"Well?" Tolan said.

"Go back inside, Abby," Clint said, and stepped down off the porch. He heard the door close.

"You ruined this for me, Adams," Tolan said. "That wasn't fair, what you did. You got Cord killed."

"He would have gotten killed sooner or later," Clint said. "For you, Johnny, it's going to be sooner."

"Says you," Tolan said, and drew.

Clint had to admit, the boy was fast. Tolan's gun was coming up when Clint's shot hit him square in the chest, same place the kid had shot Hardin—and just like Hardin, Johnny Tolan died with a look of surprise on his face.

Clint left Firecreek a week later. He and Abby decided he should wait until Duke had put some weight back on. Meanwhile, Rebecca's face healed, Petey got back on his feet, and things sort of got back to normal in town.

And Abby decided to be a doctor again.

"Although that doesn't mean I won't treat animals when they need it," she added.

The day Clint left Ansel Willis brought Clint's new horse to town for him. Clint was sad when he left, because he was leading Duke and not riding him. It was an odd situation for him.

When he came riding out of the livery Abby and Petey were there.

"What are you going to do with him?" Abby asked.

"I'll take him back to Texas," Clint said. "I have friends in Labyrinth who will take good care of him."

Petey walked over to Duke and patted his neck, saying good-bye.

"Abby," Clint asked, "what are the chances that Duke will somehow get back to normal?"

"Clint," she said, "he *is* normal for a horse his age. He's ridden a long, hard trail, and I think it's just time for him to come to the end of it."

"I guess you're right," Clint said. He looked back at the big black gelding, who looked him in the eye as if to say, What are you listening to her for?

Duke had always been a real special horse.

Anything was possible.

Watch for

DANGEROUS BREED

221st novel in the exciting GUNSMITH series
from Jove

Coming in May!

J. R. ROBERTS
THE GUNSMITH

__THE GUNSMITH #197:	APACHE RAID	0-515-12293-9/$4.99
__THE GUNSMITH #198:	THE LADY KILLERS	0-515-12303-X/$4.99
__THE GUNSMITH #199:	DENVER DESPERADOES	0-515-12341-2/$4.99
__THE GUNSMITH #200:	THE JAMES BOYS	0-515-12357-9/$4.99
__THE GUNSMITH #201:	THE GAMBLER	0-515-12373-0/$4.99
__THE GUNSMITH #202:	VIGILANTE JUSTICE	0-515-12393-5/$4.99
__THE GUNSMITH #203:	DEAD MAN'S BLUFF	0-515-12414-1/$4.99
__THE GUNSMITH #204:	WOMEN ON THE RUN	0-515-12438-9/$4.99
__THE GUNSMITH #205:	THE GAMBLER'S GIRL	0-515-12451-6/$4.99
__THE GUNSMITH #206:	LEGEND OF THE PIASA BIRD	0-515-12469-9/$4.99
__THE GUNSMITH #207:	KANSAS CITY KILLING	0-515-12486-9/$4.99
__THE GUNSMITH #208:	THE LAST BOUNTY	0-515-12512-1/$4.99
__THE GUNSMITH #209:	DEATH TIMES FIVE	0-515-12520-2/$4.99
__THE GUNSMITH #210:	MAXIMILIAN'S TREASURE	0-515-12534-2/$4.99
__THE GUNSMITH #211:	SON OF A GUNSMITH	0-515-12557-1/$4.99
__THE GUNSMITH #212:	FAMILY FEUD	0-515-12573-3/$4.99
__THE GUNSMITH #213:	STRANGLER'S VENDETTA	0-515-12615-2/$4.99
__THE GUNSMITH #214:	THE BORTON FAMILY GAME	0-515-12661-6/$4.99
__THE GUNSMITH #215:	SHOWDOWN AT DAYLIGHT	0-515-12688-8/$4.99
__THE GUNSMITH #216:	THE MAN FROM PECULIAR	0-515-12708-6/$4.99
__THE GUNSMITH #217:	AMBUSH AT BLACK ROCK	0-515-12735-3/$4.99
__THE GUNSMTIH #218:	THE CLEVELAND CONNECTION	0-515-12756-6/$4.99
__THE GUNSMITH #219:	THE BROTHEL INSPECTOR	0-515-12771-X/$4.99
__THE GUNSMITH #220:	END OF THE TRAIL	0-515-12791-4/$4.99
__THE GUNSMITH #221:	DANGEROUS BREED (5/00)	0-515-12809-0/$4.99

Prices slightly higher in Canada

Payable in U.S. funds only. No cash/COD accepted. Postage & handling: U.S./CAN. $2.75 for one book, $1.00 for each additional, not to exceed $6.75; Int'l $5.00 for one book, $1.00 each additional. We accept Visa, Amex, MC ($10.00 min.), checks ($15.00 fee for returned checks) and money orders. Call 800-788-6262 or 201-933-9292, fax 201-896-8569; refer to ad # 206 (1/00)

Penguin Putnam Inc.
P.O. Box 12289, Dept. B
Newark, NJ 07101-5289
Please allow 4-6 weeks for delivery.
Foreign and Canadian delivery 6-8 weeks.

Bill my: ❑ Visa ❑ MasterCard ❑ Amex _____ (expires)
Card# _____
Signature _____

Bill to:
Name _____
Address _____ City _____
State/ZIP _____ Daytime Phone # _____

Ship to:
Name _____ Book Total $ _____
Address _____ Applicable Sales Tax $ _____
City _____ Postage & Handling $ _____
State/ZIP _____ Total Amount Due $ _____

This offer subject to change without notice.

JAKE LOGAN
TODAY'S HOTTEST ACTION WESTERN!

☐ SLOCUM AND THE MINER'S JUSTICE #235	0-515-12371-4/$4.99
☐ SLOCUM AT HELL'S ACRE #236	0-515-12391-9/$4.99
☐ SLOCUM AND THE WOLF HUNT #237	0-515-12413-3/$4.99
☐ SLOCUM AND THE BARONESS #238	0-515-12436-2/$4.99
☐ SLOCUM AND THE COMANCHE PRINCESS #239	0-515-12449-4/$4.99
☐ SLOCUM AND THE LIVE OAK BOYS #240	0-515-12467-2/$4.99
☐ SLOCUM #241: SLOCUM AND THE BIG THREE	0-515-12484-2/$4.99
☐ SLOCUM #242: SLOCUM AT SCORPION BEND	0-515-12510-5/$4.99
☐ SLOCUM AND THE BUFFALO HUNTER #243	0-515-12518-0/$4.99
☐ SLOCUM AND THE YELLOW ROSE OF TEXAS #244	0-515-12532-6/$4.99
☐ SLOCUM AND THE LADY FROM ABILINE #245	0-515-12555-5/$4.99
☐ SLOCUM GIANT: SLOCUM AND THE THREE WIVES	0-515-12569-5/$5.99
☐ SLOCUM AND THE CATTLE KING #246	0-515-12571-7/$4.99
☐ SLOCUM #247: DEAD MAN'S SPURS	0-515-12613-6/$4.99
☐ SLOCUM #248: SHOWDOWN AT SHILOH	0-515-12659-4/$4.99
☐ SLOCUM AND THE KETCHEM GANG #249	0-515-12686-1/$4.99
☐ SLOCUM AND THE JERSEY LILY #250	0-515-12706-X/$4.99
☐ SLOCUM AND THE GAMBLER'S WOMAN #251	0-515-12733-7/$4.99
☐ SLOCUM AND THE GUNRUNNERS #252	0-515-12754-X/$4.99
☐ SLOCUM AND THE NEBRASKA STORM #253	0-515-12769-8/$4.99
☐ SLOCUM'S CLOSE CALL #254	0-515-12789-2/$4.99
☐ SLOCUM #255: SLOCUM AND THE UNDERTAKER (5/00)	0-515-12807-4/$4.99

Prices slightly higher in Canada

Payable in U.S. funds only. No cash/COD accepted. Postage & handling: U.S./CAN. $2.75 for one book, $1.00 for each additional, not to exceed $6.75; Int'l $5.00 for one book, $1.00 each additional. We accept Visa, Amex, MC ($10.00 min.), checks ($15.00 fee for returned checks) and money orders. Call 800-788-6262 or 201-933-9292, fax 201-896-8569; refer to ad # 202 (1/00)

Penguin Putnam Inc.
P.O. Box 12289, Dept. B
Newark, NJ 07101-5289
Please allow 4-6 weeks for delivery.
Foreign and Canadian delivery 6-8 weeks.

Bill my: ☐ Visa ☐ MasterCard ☐ Amex _____(expires)
Card# _____
Signature _____

Bill to:

Name _____
Address _____ City _____
State/ZIP _____ Daytime Phone # _____

Ship to:

Name _____ Book Total $ _____
Address _____ Applicable Sales Tax $ _____
City _____ Postage & Handling $ _____
State/ZIP _____ Total Amount Due $ _____

This offer subject to change without notice.

Explore the exciting Old West with one of the men who made it wild!

___ LONGARM AND THE NEVADA NYMPHS #240 0-515-12411-7/$4.99
___ LONGARM AND THE COLORADO COUNTERFEITER #241
0-515-12437-0/$4.99
___ LONGARM GIANT #18: LONGARM AND THE DANISH DAMES
0-515-12435-4/$5.50
___ LONGARM AND THE RED-LIGHT LADIES #242 0-515-12450-8/$4.99
___ LONGARM AND THE KANSAS JAILBIRD #243 0-515-12468-0/$4.99
___ LONGARM #244: LONGARM AND THE DEVIL'S SISTER
0-515-12485-0/$4.99
___ LONGARM #245: LONGARM AND THE VANISHING VIRGIN
0-515-12511-3/$4.99
___ LONGARM AND THE CURSED CORPSE #246 0-515-12519-9/$4.99
___ LONGARM AND THE LADY FROM TOMBSTONE #247
0-515-12533-4/$4.99
___ LONGARM AND THE WRONGED WOMAN #248 0-515-12556-3/$4.99
___ LONGARM AND THE SHEEP WAR #249 0-515-12572-5/$4.99
___ LONGARM AND THE CHAIN GANG WOMEN #250 0-515-12614-4/$4.99
___ LONGARM AND THE DIARY OF MADAME VELVET #251
0-515-12660-8/$4.99
___ LONGARM AND THE FOUR CORNERS GANG #249 0-515-12687-X/$4.99
___ LONGARM IN THE VALLEY OF SIN #253 0-515-12707-8/$4.99
___ LONGARM AND THE REDHEAD'S RANSOM #254 0-515-12734-5/$4.99
___ LONGARM AND THE MUSTANG MAIDEN #255 0-515-12755-8/$4.99
___ LONGARM AND THE DYNAMITE DAMSEL #256 0-515-12770-1/$4.99
___ LONGARM AND THE NEVADA BELLYDANCER #257 0-515-12790-6/$4.99
___ LONGARM #258: LONGARM AND THE PISTOLERO
PRINCESS (5/00) 0-515-12808-2/$4.99

Prices slightly higher in Canada

Payable in U.S. funds only. No cash/COD accepted. Postage & handling: U.S./CAN. $2.75 for one book, $1.00 for each additional, not to exceed $6.75; Int'l $5.00 for one book, $1.00 each additional. We accept Visa, Amex, MC ($10.00 min.), checks ($15.00 fee for returned checks) and money orders. Call 800-788-6262 or 201-933-9292, fax 201-896-8569; refer to ad # 201 (1/00)

Penguin Putnam Inc.
P.O. Box 12289, Dept. B
Newark, NJ 07101-5289
Please allow 4-6 weeks for delivery.
Foreign and Canadian delivery 6-8 weeks.

Bill my: ❑ Visa ❑ MasterCard ❑ Amex _____ (expires)
Card# _____
Signature _____

Bill to:
Name _____
Address _____ City _____
State/ZIP _____ Daytime Phone # _____

Ship to:
Name _____ Book Total $ _____
Address _____ Applicable Sales Tax $ _____
City _____ Postage & Handling $ _____
State/ZIP _____ Total Amount Due $ _____

This offer subject to change without notice.

From the creators of Longarm!

BUSHWHACKERS

They were the most brutal gang of cutthroats ever assembled. And during the Civil War, they sought justice outside of the law—paying back every Yankee raid with one of their own. They rode hard, shot straight, and had their way with every willin' woman west of the Mississippi. No man could stop them. No woman could resist them. And no Yankee stood a chance of living when Quantrill's Raiders rode into town...

Win and Joe Coulter became the two most wanted men in the West. And they learned just how sweet—and deadly—revenge could be...

BUSHWHACKERS by B. J. Lanagan
0-515-12102-9/$4.99

BUSHWHACKERS #2: REBEL COUNTY
0-515-12142-8/$4.99

BUSHWHACKERS#3:
THE KILLING EDGE 0-515-12177-0/$4.99

BUSHWHACKERS #4:
THE DYING TOWN 0-515-12232-7/$4.99

BUSHWHACKERS #5:
MEXICAN STANDOFF 0-515-12263-7/$4.99

BUSHWHACKERS #6:
EPITAPH 0-515-12290-4/$4.99

BUSHWHACKERS #7:
A TIME FOR KILLING 0-515-12574-1/$4.99

BUSHWHACKERS #8:
DEATH PASS 0-515-12658-6/$4.99

BUSHWHACKERS #9:
HANGMAN'S DROP 0-515-12731-0/$4.99

Prices slightly higher in Canada

Payable in U.S. funds only. No cash/COD accepted. Postage & handling: U.S./CAN. $2.75 for one book, $1.00 for each additional, not to exceed $6.75; Int'l $5.00 for one book, $1.00 each additional. We accept Visa, Amex, MC ($10.00 min.), checks ($15.00 fee for returned checks) and money orders. Call 800-788-6262 or 201-933-9292, fax 201-896-8569; refer to ad # 705 (1/00)

Penguin Putnam Inc.
P.O. Box 12289, Dept. B
Newark, NJ 07101-5289
Please allow 4-6 weeks for delivery.
Foreign and Canadian delivery 6-8 weeks.

Bill my: ☐ Visa ☐ MasterCard ☐ Amex _____ (expires)
Card# _____
Signature _____

Bill to:
Name _____
Address _____ City _____
State/ZIP _____ Daytime Phone # _____

Ship to:
Name _____ Book Total $ _____
Address _____ Applicable Sales Tax $ _____
City _____ Postage & Handling $ _____
State/ZIP _____ Total Amount Due $ _____

This offer subject to change without notice.